Lucy:
A Prickle Creek Romance

ANNIE SEATON

Home to the Outback: Book 1

LUCY

This book is a work of fiction. Names, characters, places, and incidents are the product of the author's imagination or are used fictitiously. Any resemblance to actual events, locales, or persons, living or dead, is coincidental.

Previously Published in the US as Her Outback Cowboy (2017)

All rights reserved

ISBN: 9781923048645

PROLOGUE

Sydney: Sebastian Richards

Sebastian Richards put down his camera and pulled the buzzing phone from his pocket. 'You can take a break, kids.' He forced a smile to his face as he gestured to the mother of the small children he was shooting for the department store catalogue. The little boy poked his tongue out at Sebastian as he ran past, and he thanked his lucky stars for the call that had interrupted the photo shoot from hell. The little fiend's sister aimed a kick at Seb's ankles and stood there staring at him.

God, I hate working with kids.

He was so preoccupied watching for the kicking feet of the child from hell that he didn't look at the screen before he pressed answer. 'Seb Richards.'

His blood ran cold as he heard the voice on the other end.

The last person he would expect to call him. He turned away from the small girl, not caring if he got kicked to kingdom come. It would be preferable to talking to his grandmother.

'Sebastian.'

'Hello, Gran.'

'I want you all to come home.'

'All who?'

'Don't be smart, boy. You and your cousins.'

'Sorry, Gran. I'm at work. I'll call you back.'

He disconnected before she could reply and shoved the phone back into his pocket.

'Sorry, Mrs Armitage. That was . . . er, business. I have to go. Take your kids out for some lunch, and we'll meet back here at two o'clock.'

He grabbed his camera and tripod and ran down the stairs. If he was quick, he could get to the office on the next floor before the old bat called Lucy.

***

Sydney: Jemima Smythe

Across town, Jemima Smythe ignored her ringing phone as the stylist touched up the last of her makeup. She sat straight, the clinging blue silk of the formal dress whispering against her bare legs. The fashion parade was at the famous Sydney Opera House, and everyone was on their best behaviour. This was her chance to get to Paris; she'd heard there was a talent scout from an agency in the audience today.

'You're up next, Jemima,' Roger called. Next on the catwalk, and if she answered this call, she'd miss her cue, and Roger, the volatile stage manager, would go troppo. Normally, Jemima worked on being serene and presenting a calm exterior to the world. It was amazing how many favours—and indeed extra jobs—she'd picked up because of her reputation as an easy-to-get-on-with model, not a prima donna, no matter how hard the shoot or the day on the catwalk was.

The stylist put his makeup brush down. 'You're right to go. Perfect, as usual. And listen, the word is the guy from the agency is in the front row. Go get 'em, babe.'

Jemima glanced down at the screen, and all serenity fled. A familiar number flashed on the screen.

Oh, bloody hell, why is Gran calling? What was wrong?

Not now. She had to stay calm. This was her chance to hit the big time.

***

London: Liam Smythe

The high-pitched chorus of Queen's *Bohemian Rhapsody* shattered Liam Smythe's sleep. He jerked awake and fumbled for his phone in the dark. He glanced at the red digital figures of his watch sitting on the bedside table as he grabbed his mobile and pressed it to his ear.

What the hell? It was only three a.m. And where was he? Another bloody hotel in what town? Liam had to think for a minute before he remembered he was in London. In his own bed in his apartment.

God, he hated calls that came in the middle of the night. They were always bad news.

'Liam Smythe.' He cleared his throat, his voice gravelly from the one too many drinks he'd had when the news desk staff had wandered down to the West End after last night's shift.

'Is that my favourite grandson?' A sweet voice chimed over the line, all the way from down under, all the way from the Pilliga Scrub in the Australian outback, to be precise.

Over ten thousand miles away from his safe and quiet apartment on the bank of the Thames River in London.

But Liam wasn't fooled. That sweet little voice belonged to a woman with a backbone of steel. He sat up straighter and ran a hand through his hair as if she could see him.

'Hey, Gran.' He leaned back against the bedhead and reached for a cigarette before remembering he'd given them up last month. 'Is everything okay?'

***

Sydney: Lucy Peterkin

Lucy Peterkin rested the mobile phone between her chin and shoulder, keeping both hands on the computer keyboard before she answered the call beeping. Her eyes were focused on the screen as she put the final finishing touch on her project. She leaned forward, adding a bright red swirl to each corner of the graphic. This was some of her best work yet, and her boss, Caleb, was going to love it; she smiled with satisfaction before she let go of the mouse and hit the answer button on the phone.

'No, Luce, don't do it. Don't pick up.' Her head flew up as Seb, her colleague, cousin and best friend in the whole world, ran into the small booth tucked into the back corner of the large open-plan office.

Caleb, their trendsetter boss, said it was important for everyone to have their own creative space. Yeah, sure; what it meant was he could watch everyone work from his office up in the loft above the large open floor. And he pushed them hard. But it worked for Lucy, and usually, she didn't mind the lack of privacy—or the close supervision. All Caleb wanted was a fair day's work from his staff. And he got it from her. Lucy loved her job, and she loved living in the city, even though her current apartment was old and tacky.

She sighed; she had to finish this presentation today. All afternoon, there had been interruption after interruption, ringing phones, and now Seb was bursting in, full of instructions. She lifted her chin, tempted to poke her tongue out at her bossy cousin as she answered the call. He shook his head and put his hands over his face; Lucy bit back a groan as she heard the sweet voice and slumped into the chair on the other side of her desk.

Seb shook his head. 'I tried to tell you,' he mouthed.

ANNIE SEATON

CHAPTER 1

Lucy hung up the call and crossed her red, polka-dotted tights-clad legs. She pretended to ignore Sebastian, and he frowned as she flicked an imaginary speck of dust from her red knee-length boots.

'You are the softest touch, Luce. I cannot believe you! Correct me if I'm wrong but did you agree with her? Bloody hell.'

'Oh, are you still here, Seb?' She would play the cranky card. She'd seen his eye roll when she'd disconnected and then had decided that ignoring him was the best strategy. Sweetness didn't work in their family; they'd all learned that very early. And Seb could be a spoiled brat.

'You know full well I'm here, Lucy. Don't be a smart arse.'

'So not Luce anymore? I'm Lucy now?' She clicked the mouse and turned back to face him. All six foot-six of her cousin, dressed in black as usual. 'Okay, so what's your problem this time, Sebastian Richards? You're always trying to boss me around and it's way past time that you accept we're equal employees here at the agency.'

LUCY

'It's nothing to do with work, as you well know.' He gestured to the phone. 'I heard you talking to *her*. I told you not to answer it.'

Lucy leaned back and folded her arms, her voice rising. 'And since when do I listen to you?'

'Not when you should, that's for bloody sure.' Seb ran his hand through his long hair, and Lucy softened. He really was upset.

'Did I really hear you agree to spend your summer holiday out in the Pilliga scrub with the old battleaxe?'

'You did. And don't call my grandmother an old battleaxe.'

'*Our* grandmother.' He lifted his head, and his eyes were sad as he forced a smile.

'And you can't talk; you're as hard as nails.' Lucy pointed at her cousin and ignored his plastered-on smile. She'd seen any sympathy he'd had for her disappear the instant she'd agreed to go home to see Gran and Pop.

'Of course, I'll come, Gran,' Lucy had said. 'I hate to think of you out there at Prickle Creek by yourself.' A note of worry crept into her voice. 'Pop is okay, isn't he?'

'Y… e … es. He's fine.'

'But?'

'Nothing.'

'Really?'

Sebastian shook his head when Lucy told him Gran had been teary. 'The old battleaxe has you sucked in, hook.'

'Sebastian. Stop it. They've only got us, remember. We're all they've got left. Do I have to remind you of that?'

'No, of course, you don't, but the old cow will use us for whatever purpose she has in mind. And you fell for it, Lucy. Hook, line, and sinker.'

'Bugger off, Seb. There are times when I don't like you very much.'

But instead of leaving, her cousin stood and crossed to the window overlooking Sydney Harbour. Lucy followed his gaze out over the harbour; she'd been so busy all day she'd paid scant attention to the day outside. When she'd left her apartment this morning, the weather had been clear and bright and it had put her in a good mood for the work she'd had ahead of her. But she always carried an umbrella in this fickle coastal weather.

As she'd walked through the Rocks this morning, the concierges of the five-star hotels she passed doffed their hats and smiled at her. She knew them all by name, and most mornings when she got off the bus at the end of George

Street, she would linger to chat and was often late to work, much to Caleb's displeasure.

'Morning, Miss Lucy.'

'Morning, Erwin, has that daughter of yours had her baby yet?'

'Morning, Lucy.'

'Hey Reggie, how was the football game last night?'

It always brightened her day as she got off the bus and walked through the Rocks to the office.

'Love those red polka dots.' Erwin's grin had been wider than usual this morning as he'd looked at her outfit. Lucy liked to make a statement with her dress. It made her feel as though she was a part of the vibrant city. She felt like she belonged to the arty graphic design community at the top of town.

'Thank you, Erwin.' She'd smiled back at him and waved her frilly umbrella. 'My tights match my umbrella.'

He'd chuckled as she twirled around, the frills on the edge of the red-spotted umbrella fluttering in the stiff breeze.

'I noticed.'

When she'd been at high school, Gran's neighbour's son—Garth Mackenzie—had teased her about the colourful, zany clothes Lucy had worn to school every day. It hadn't taken long for her to realise he'd only teased her so he could find an excuse to talk to her. She smiled: he'd never known she'd chosen the crazy outfits so he would take notice of her. Last she'd heard, Garth had married a girl from the outback and moved to a cotton farm. He'd been her first love and the guy who had stolen her teenage heart. Lucy pushed away the little feeling of sadness that rippled through her.

As she'd walked along the harbour, she hummed one of the country and western songs she and Garth had sung together when they'd been a couple.

'And I'm crazy for lovin' you,' she'd mouthed the final words of the song as heavy clouds scudded across the sky over the harbour, matching the blue mood that had suddenly descended on her. The threatening rain—she could smell it in the strong southerly wind snapping the colourful banners on the Museum of Contemporary across the square—was very different to the dry and dusty outback of her teenage years.

'Lucy!' Sebastian's voice broke into her daydreaming. 'Just because her kids are gone doesn't give her rights to the next generation. You know what a controlling witch she is. She wants something from us, and you know it. That's why I wouldn't talk to her when she rang. I tried to warn you.' He stared at her, his dark brown eyes narrowed in a frown. 'Come on, Lucy. Think about it. The farm! Flies, smelly cattle, prickles and red dust. You hated it!'

Lucy's attitude towards the farm had been a standing joke in the family when they'd been kids and visited Gran and Pop's property. Dad loved to tell the story of her standing in a cow pat when she was about ten years old, looking down her young nose with disdain.

'I so hate farms,' he'd mimicked her perfectly for years afterwards. 'When I grow up, I'm going to live in an apartment in the middle of the city.' So no one had been surprised when Lucy had hightailed it to the big smoke straight after high school.

Lucy had settled into city life and when tragedy had hit the family, Dad had moved to Canada. He'd left within a year of the accident. Mum and her two sisters had been killed in a car crash on their much-awaited European holiday. It was only a year later that Dad had had a heart attack and died.

A broken heart, Lily liked to think. She knew how much her parents had loved each other and when Mum had gone, Dad had been utterly lost without her.

So, Lucy had her new life, far away from her family, until Seb arrived in the city when he came home from Europe.

The Pilliga Scrub hadn't been home to any of the cousins for a long time.

University, overseas trips, and Lucy's career as a graphic artist had taken precedence over going back to Prickle Creek, the small western New South Wales town where they had all grown up. Prickle Creek Farm was fifty kilometres west of town, and she hadn't been back since she left when she was eighteen.

She turned to Sebastian, and her voice shook. 'Not going back had nothing to do with the . . . with Gran.' It was still hard to speak of it even though it had been five years. 'It's the thought of going back to town, knowing Mum isn't there anymore, that kept me in the city.' She held out a hand to Seb. 'It's time we all went back. They're getting old. We can't leave it till it's too late.'

He shook his head.

'Come on, Seb, memories can't kill us. I'm going to do as she asked. And two weeks of keeping Gran company won't kill me,' she said as Seb looked at her in disbelief. 'Or you.'

'So, what does she want you to do? I ended the call before she could tell me that she wanted me out there too. Said I'd call her back later, but I'm not going to.' Seb's lips were set in a mutinous line.

'Pop's in hospital in Prickle Creek.'

That got his attention, and his eyes narrowed. 'I didn't know the old codger was sick.'

'It's nothing dire; he's having a knee replacement, and Gran needs a hand on the property.'

'So what are you going to be doing?' A smile cracked his face. 'Gawd, Luce, you hated the farm when we were kids. I can't see you helping out in the paddocks. Liam, Jemmy and I loved it, but you? I can still see your nose wrinkled up from the stench. 'Eww, smelly cattle!' I remember you used to compare the cattle yards to the Bog of Eternal Stench from that movie you loved.'

'*Labyrinth*, and I won't be going anywhere near the yards. I'm simply helping Gran out with the cooking for the contract workers. I won't have to go anywhere near the cows. Or out on the farm at all.'

'Cattle. Steers and heifers,' Seb said distractedly. 'Cows are in dairies.' He frowned and stared through the window behind her head. 'It's wheat harvest time, if I have the right farm calendar in my memory still. There'll be a dozen men working day and night with bloody big headers in those never-ending paddocks.'

'I'm impressed. You still know the farm lingo.' She injected sarcasm into her voice and waved her hand. 'Cows, cattle, whatever.'

'You know what they say.'

'What?'

'You can take the boy out of the country but—'

'Oh, puh-leeze.' Finally, Lucy let out a giggle. 'Come on, Seb. Be a sport, come with me. I can work while I'm out there.'

'Nup. No way. She's up to something, and I'm not going anywhere near her. You might be naïve, but I know dear old Granny, and she wants more than a cook.'

'Be kind. The four of us lost our mothers, but don't forget Gran and Pa lost their three daughters.' Her voice trembled a little as she managed to put the past tragedy into words. It was something that they didn't speak about. 'No parent should lose a child, but they lost all three of their daughters in one accident. And we all left and followed our own lives.'

'Yeah, but she wants something. Why the heck would she want us out there all of a sudden? I mean, okay, Pop might be having a knee operation, but why the heck would she need all of us out there at the same time?'

'Maybe she misses us all and needs a hand on the place?'

'And a graphic designer slash copywriter and a photographer from the city are going to do cattle work in the middle of nowhere. With a fashion model and a journalist. Give me a break.' He stood and put his hands on his hips. 'She can afford to hire someone. They're loaded.'

'Don't you feel one bit guilty that we've avoided them?'

He shook his head, and Lucy suppressed a groan. She wasn't going to let Sebastian see how nervous she was about going out there. 'Well, I'm going. I can cook and someone can come and collect it from the house. I won't be leaving the air-conditioned kitchen.'

'And what about your big campaign? It's all you could talk about—how busy you were going to be till Christmas.'

'I'll work at night.'

'If she lets you. She'll be manipulating you like she always does.' He shook his head and leaned against her desk. His shirt hung trendily, loose over his designer jeans. 'Call me if it gets too bad, and I'll come up with an emergency to bring you back to Sydney.'

'If I do call you, it will be to get your butt out there and help. Although Gran did say Liam has agreed to come home too.' Lucy watched Sebastian carefully as she played her last card. She didn't want to go, and, yeah, he was right; she was a soft touch, but it was the right thing to do.

'What? You mean Wonder Boy, the world-famous journalist, is coming home from London? Not only will I come up and see that, but I'd eat my hat and run around the paddock stark bollocky naked if Liam comes home.'

'I'll hold you to that. Jemima's coming too,' she said quietly. 'Gran was sure she was. Three of us, and if you agree, that'll make all four.'

LUCY

'Bullshit.' Seb pushed himself off her desk and headed for the door. He turned around and stared at her, his eyes intense.

'Get out of here,' she said. 'If I'm going to the Pilliga Scrub, I need to get some work done before I go.'

Sebastian wandered out, but not before Lucy saw the guilty look that flashed across his face as he turned away.

CHAPTER 2

'Thanks, Jim. I'll leave you to get cooking.' Garth Mackenzie sniffed appreciatively as the aroma of beef stew filled the kitchen adjacent to the workmen's quarters. 'I might eat down here with the men once the harvesting starts. Smells bloody good.'

'You're welcome, boss. There'll be plenty to go around.' The contracted cook had settled into the old building at the back of the farm, and he was ready to feed the workers when the harvesting started later in the week. Garth had bought two huge freezers and a large oven for the old shearing shed when his parents had left the farm. From the look of the pots bubbling on the stove and the aroma of baking bread coming from the oven, his workers were going to be fed well this harvest.

He whistled for Jack and waited till his old dog caught him up before walking along the eastern boundary fence and checking the dam levels. Once he was done, he'd saddle up his horse and move the cattle to the back paddock, and then he'd check the dams on the other side of the farm. It had been so dry he was going to have to pump some water from the water table beneath the farm if it didn't rain soon. He looked over at Prickle Creek Farm and wondered how old Harry Bellamy was getting on. He'd been limping around for the past month or so. There was no point going over there to offer to help out. Since Garth had had words with Helena about the cattle, he'd noticed a padlock go up on the gate that joined the properties—the gate that had once been a meeting place for his and Lucy Peterkin's midnight swims in the dam. Garth shook his head; those weeks at the end of high school, before he'd left for university, had been some of the best days of his life.

Those days were long gone now, and the family farm had been handed to him. Lucy had left town, and he often wondered where she'd ended up. He stood looking out over the waving heads of wheat, golden and ready to be harvested. The rich red coats of the Hereford cattle were glossy in the late morning sun, and he smiled as they munched on the rich pasture beside the wheat paddock. The sky was a brilliant blue, and the forecast of rain looked like it wasn't going to eventuate. Satisfaction filled him; he'd worked hard to get himself to this position, and the dividends were beginning to show. It had been worth every one of the six years he'd spent away from the family farm. It was so good to be back; he didn't intend to go anywhere else for a long time. This wheat harvest was set to be the best one in years. His parents were settled down on the coast, and he was his own boss for the first time in his life.

Life was bloody good.

Maybe it was time for a trip into Prickle Creek Returned Soldiers' Club—affectionately known to locals as the R.S.L. or the rissole—to catch up with some of his friends one Friday night. It could get a bit lonely at times. Jack nudged at his thigh, and Garth reached down and absentmindedly rubbed his head. 'Come on, old fella. We'll go and get you some dinner, and then you can spend the afternoon sleeping in the shade. Some of us have to work, you know.'

***

A week after Gran's call, Lucy set off from Sydney on Friday morning just after dawn. Even that early, the traffic was chaotic in the city as commuters headed to work. She sighed as she caught red light after red light. Finally, she was out of the city and heading up the M1. She turned off the new Hunter Express bypass and onto the Golden Highway, and soon, the green paddocks of the horse studs of the upper Hunter Valley were flashing by. Peace and serenity replaced the angst caused by the city traffic, and she turned off the air conditioning and slid the window down, taking a deep breath of fresh country air.

After three more hours on the road, a couple of coffee stops, and finally, she swung into the car park of Prickle Creek Health Centre. Climbing out of the car, she stretched her arms. The trees lining the path were in full bloom, and the gardens were redolent with the sweet fragrance of full-blown roses. Fat yellow blooms nodded their heavy heads in the hospital garden, soaking up the last of the summer sun. The health centre was nothing like the multi-storey hospitals in Sydney, and even though she didn't recognise any of the nurses on the desk, they all smiled a friendly greeting. There are some things about the country that left the city for dead, Lucy thought.

Pop was sitting up in bed and teasing one of the nurses as the young girl giggled and propped up his pillows. He always had a joke or a story wherever he was, and Lucy knew it was his way of coping with the grief that had consumed the family after the tragedy. One split second, one wrong decision by a drunk driver, and their family had shattered.

'Did I tell you the one about the doctor and the—'

'Hey, Pop.' She walked into the ward and received a grateful glance from the young nurse. 'You haven't been annoying the staff, have you, you old joker?'

She looked down at her bag, pretending not to see the tears that filled Pop's eyes. She fought them back; he looked tired and gaunt.

'Lucy, come and give a sick old man a kiss.' It was as though she'd been there only the other day, and Pop didn't mention that she'd been away for all those years. She drew in a breath as the comforting scrape of his grey whiskers brushed her chin when she leaned in to kiss his cheek.

'Sweetheart, it's wonderful to see you. Gran tells me you're going to stay and help out?'

'Yep. I'm heading for the farm now. My friend Julie asked me to visit if I ever came to town, but I'll catch up with her another time.'

'Got a husband and two kids, I hear.' Her grandfather flicked a sly look her way. 'Might get you a bit clucky, love.'

'Don't go getting any ideas, you old rascal.' Lucy straightened the cotton blanket before she sat in the plastic chair next to the bed. 'I'm a career girl through and through.'

He shook his head. 'You'll come back to the country one day. It's in your blood. We missed you, love.'

Lucy wasn't going to get into an argument, especially when he was still in the hospital. She pointed to his knee. 'So what's with the operation?'

'Gawd, nothing much. Just my rheumy old knee where I got it caught in the cattle crush when you were little. They're going to give me a plastic one tomorrow. Bloody wonders never cease!'

'That's good news. You had me worried. You'll be back home and on horseback before you know it.'

'I wish,' he said sadly. 'Things have changed a lot, Lucy. It's not like it used to be at the farm.'

Lucy tried to swallow the big lump that seemed to be stuck in her throat. 'I'd better get going. I'll come back and see you tomorrow. Okay?'

Her grandfather turned to her with a frown. 'You watch out on that road out to the farm. I don't want you hitting a roo.'

'They'll all be asleep in the shade by the time I reach the turn-off. I'll be fine.'

She tooted the horn as she left the hospital. She knew he'd be waiting for it.

Lucy rolled into her grandparents' farm late in the afternoon. Nerves skittered in her stomach as she parked her car outside the familiar farmhouse. As she'd driven through town and out along the road to the farm, every paddock and every road held memories that she'd buried deep.

Gran met her at the door, wiping her hands on a floury apron, her iron-grey hair pulled into a severe bun. Guilt flooded through Lucy. Her grandmother looked thin—and *old*.

'It's so good to see you, dear. It's way past time for our family to be together.' Gran held her close for a couple of seconds, and Lucy fought the tears that threatened. 'Is that Sebastian going to come too?'

'Maybe. You know Seb. Always chasing another adventure with his camera.' She stepped back and held her grandmother's cold hands.

'Although he's settled down a lot since he's been at the agency with me. What about the others?'

'Jemima and Liam will be here on Monday.'

'Really?' The hard lump in her chest eased as she thought of the all—almost all—being together again. 'Then I'm sure I'll be able to entice Sebastian up here.' She looked curiously at Gran. 'Why did you call us all home, Gran?'

'Come away into the kitchen and let me have a look at you. I've got some scones that are just about due out of the oven.' Gran's English accent was always stronger when she was emotional. Lucy put her bag in the hall and followed her grandmother to the back of the rambling old farmstead. She put her head down and ignored the many family photos lining the floral-sprigged wallpaper all the way from the door, along the hall, to the kitchen.

The kitchen was the same as ever, and a pang of nostalgic memory ripped through Lucy; she drew in her breath at the almost physical pain. Even though she'd hated farm life, the days she'd spent here at the farm with her three cousins had been a huge part of her childhood—and such fun. She'd learned to cook on that stove; she and Jemmy had made lamingtons for school fetes with Gran, and they'd pickled onions for the

CWA stall at the annual agricultural show until their skin and hair smelled like vinegar. The same yellow gingham curtains that had always been there still graced the window above the sink and the huge scrubbed wooden table where they'd had many a Christmas dinner together took pride of place in the middle of the flagged stone floor. Trinkets and knick-knacks filled the old dresser beside the back door. Nothing had changed apart from two shiny new chest freezers Lucy could see in the little room off the back porch.

'Ralph!' Lucy crouched down at the dog basket beside the door and looked up at Gran. A familiar black and white head lifted and she reached out to pat the old dog. 'Oh my God, it is Ralphie, isn't it, Gran?'

'It is.' Her grandmother pursed her lips. 'Although I don't know why that silly old fool of your grandfather insists on keeping him. He's way past his working life. Not good for anything apart from eating. Waste of space.'

A glimmer of disquiet ran through Lucy; Sebastian was right in some ways. Gran had been raised in a family where 'waste not, want not' was the code, and her attitude could be hard at times. But it wasn't for her to judge; they didn't know how hard it had been in the years when Gran and Pop had tried to build up a rundown farm into a profitable concern.

'Come on, Gran. You don't mean that.' She tickled the dog beneath his chin, and he gave a soft woof, his brown eyes looking at her lovingly. 'See, he remembers me.'

'Just looking for food.' Gran gave an impatient harrumph. 'Come away with you.' She put her hands on Lucy's shoulders and looked away from her.

Lucy looked down at her, but Gran was staring through the window, her lips set.

'I think Seb's sorry he had a fight with you, Gran. But you know him; he'll never admit he did the wrong thing.' Lucy laid it on thick to try and win Gran over. 'He's not gay, you know.'

'I wouldn't care if he was gay or whatever he wanted to be. He knows how ridiculous and what a waste of money I think that stupid parade is. All the money goes to the city, and poor communities like ours struggle out here. Anyway, enough of this chin-wagging. I've got work to do.' Gran pointed to the table before she reached for an oven mitt. 'Get yourself an apron, and you can help me get the scones ready. And don't forget to wash your hands.'

Lucy hid a smile as she did as she was told and crossed to the sink.

They worked quietly together as Gran pulled three dozen scones from the large oven. Lucy lifted the hot scones onto the wire trays to cool, and Gran whipped the cream to put into the containers for the workers, along with small containers of homemade jam.

'There, all ready for tomorrow morning's smoko.' Gran stepped back and looked at Lucy. 'You must be tired after that long drive.'

'Just a bit.' Lucy reached up and tucked her loose hair behind her ear. 'Why did you call us all home, Gran?'

'You've got taller, Lucy.'

'I've been this tall since I was twelve years old, silly.' Lucy said with a smile. 'Don't change the subject.'

'Well, we've barely seen you since then, so what would I remember.' Gran clucked her tongue.

'So, why the summons to Prickle Creek, Gran? What's going on?'

Her grandmother waved her hand and turned to the stove and peered into the oven. 'Time for that later when you're all here. Go and have a swim in the dam, you look hot. I'll get our dinner on. It'll be nice to have company at the dinner table,' she said gruffly. 'We've got one day before the rest of the contractors arrive to finish off the harvest.'

##

Lucy slipped on her swimmers and grabbed a hat. She walked to the dam past the waving fields of golden wheat and sighed as the heat rose from the cracked brown dirt. The crop wasn't going to the mill this year; Pop had said cattle prices were up high, making the wheat crop more profitable for the farm if it was baled to feed the cattle.

'And the cattle love it, Luce.' He'd talked to her for half an hour before she'd finally got away from the hospital. His old eyes had lit up as he told her the plan for the pasture this summer. 'Wheat hay has eighteen percent protein, and the soft stems are really good for the calves.' Lucy had switched off as he rattled off figures and weights, turning back to him when he mentioned the contractors that needed to be fed. It was a big harvest this year, and more contractors were due to hit Prickle Creek with their headers the day after tomorrow. One consolation: they'd be busy feeding the extra men, and her time here would pass quickly. Sebastian was right; it was hard, and she was trying to keep the sad memories locked away. But it would be fun to catch up with Liam and Jemmy. It had been a long time since they'd all been together. She caught up with Jemmy for the occasional coffee when she had modelling jobs in Sydney, but it had been at least a year since she'd last seen her.

Spending two weeks here wouldn't be too bad. Lucy knew she'd just have to steel herself and dig deep for strength to pitch in and help. Twenty-four bloody hours a day, those machines would go up and down, the workers cocooned in their little air-conditioned cabs with earbuds blocking out the monotonous sound of the motors.

The dam was a long way from the wheat paddock but no matter where you were on the five thousand acres at harvest time, you couldn't escape that noise. The first couple of paddocks were already being cut and she waved to the contractors in the enclosed cabins of the big machines as she made her way to the dam. She stopped at the gate, reached up and pulled a small branch from a low-hanging tree, swishing it around her head to keep the flies away.

The brown water was not very enticing, but at least it was wet and sort of cool. After having a good look around the edge for snakes, Lucy kicked off her boots and walked into the water, floating as soon as she could to get her feet off the muddy bottom.

'What the heck am I doing out here?' She closed her eyes and let the warm water slide over her body. If she scrunched her eyelids tightly closed, she could imagine the translucent green waters of Hamilton Island whispering over her hot skin. Summoning up the feel of pure white sand squeaking beneath her feet and the sound of the ocean breeze rustling the palms, she let the idyllic tropical picture fill her mind for one brief moment until she opened her eyes and looked out over the golden paddocks and the red dirt road in front of her.

Hamilton Island was where she'd dreamed of spending her short summer holiday this year. Not that she really had time to take a holiday; she had a proposal to finish. The biggest lingerie company in Australia had chosen Goodbody and Grech as the company to launch their new line of sexy underwear, and the advertising manager had dropped the campaign into Lucy's willing hands; the design and the copy. A campaign that would give her advertising career an almighty push upwards.

If she could find the right image. Something new, something fresh, not like the current garbage that was being spewed out by some of the Sydney agencies.

And if I can ever get online here in the boondocks. She suspected the internet service wouldn't be too good out here; she'd tried to check her email before she'd changed into her swimmers. Even with her dongle, the connection here at Prickle Creek Farm was painfully slow.

She tilted her head back, letting the lukewarm water swish through her hair as the hot sun beat down on her face. Lucy closed her eyes as the past flashed by. Where had the years gone? And *why* had she agreed to come back so quickly?

Maybe Seb was right; maybe she'd made a huge mistake. She had so much work lined up, and Gran and Pop did have enough money to hire someone to help out.

Although the cousins had let the farm go, and had left it all up to Gran and Pop. Another ripple of guilt fluttered through her.

Lucy floated on her back and blocked out the sound of the headers as the hay was baled in the paddock across from the dam. The heat out here in the Pilliga Scrub in late summer was searing.

It was a tossup whether the heat, the flies, or the cat's-head prickles were the worst part of this landscape.

She flicked her hand in the water and kept her eyes closed as she counted the days and tried not to think of the tropical holiday she'd dreamed about. Fourteen days working her butt off in this arid, hot, and flat landscape was not a fair trade, but she'd agreed, and she'd see it through.

'Lucy Lou! I thought it was you I saw walking across the paddock.' The laconic voice pulled Lucy from her daydreaming, and she opened her mouth, spluttering as she copped a mouthful of muddy dam water.

She lowered her feet and squealed as her toes sank in the squishy mud.

'Oh, yuk! How gross,' she muttered.

Lucy knew that voice too well; her memory kicked into gear bringing back a few afternoons by the dam with Garth Mackenzie when they'd been at high school.

And wow, what memories. Her face heated, and it wasn't just the hot sun that was causing it. The outback sun hadn't been the only thing to heat the air in those days. She kept her head down as she trudged through the fine silt, trying to look unconcerned and hide how fast her heart was beating. She wondered why Grant was back here and not up north at his cotton farm. She reached the edge of the dam, grimacing as the cool mud oozed between her toes.

'Garth! It's been a long time.' Lucy managed to regain her composure and push aside the memory of him standing stark naked on that very same spot. In those steamy days, they'd not worried about swimming costumes. It was far enough from the road that there was always plenty of warning if someone came along by car or on horseback.

Garth leaned down, and his hands were strong and firm on her shoulders as he brushed his lips across her cheek. 'It surely has. What are you doing back here? Thought you'd abandoned the country for the big smoke years ago?'

'I'm here to help Gran out for a couple of weeks. Pop's in the hospital.'

'I heard that.' His gold-flecked hazel eyes held hers as he spoke quietly. 'I was sorry to hear about your mum, Lucy. I was away, and I didn't get to the funeral. It's been a tough few years for your whole family.'

'Yep, it has, but time passes and helps us heal, doesn't it?' Keeping her voice steady, Lucy squinted up at him in the bright sun. His Akubra hat shaded his chiselled face, and she stared. Garth had always been the best-looking boy at school. His eyes were always alight with laughter, and he'd been a good friend to her, both before and after their brief fling. As she gazed up at him, her mouth dropped open, and she stepped back, raising her hands. She made a square with the fingers of both her hands and captured both him and the horse through a pretend viewfinder.

'Don't move.'

'What?' His deep voice was as sexy as ever, and Lucy's creative juices kicked in, banishing the butterfly flutters. 'What's wrong?'

'You, Garth Mackenzie, are the answer to my dreams.'

Brilliant blue sky formed a backdrop for his rugged face and strong shoulders. Lucy let her eyes travel down past his shoulders to his buttoned-up shirt tucked into navy blue work pants. Scuffed boots were planted firmly in the red dust at the edge of the dam, his strong thighs outlined by the close-fitting pants. His white teeth flashed as he grinned at her, shaking his head. In the background, a shiny brown horse pawed at the ground and snuffled behind the fence.

He's perfect! The horse is perfect! The landscape is perfect!

'Where's Seb when I need him,' Lucy muttered as she lifted her gaze back to Garth's face. The perfect shot for her advertising proposal was out here at Prickle Creek, a place where she would never have thought of looking in a million years.

'Madcap as ever, Lucy-Lou?' His eyes crinkled at the edges, full of laughter and interest.

She grabbed his hands, reached over and planted a smacking kiss on his mouth. 'You, Garth Mackenzie, have solved my problem. Want to come over to the house for a cuppa and we can talk about it?'

CHAPTER 3

Garth ignored the feeling that had slammed into his chest when he thought he spotted Lucy Peterkin crossing the paddock to the dam. He'd blinked, dropped the wire strainer and rubbed a grimy hand across his eyes. For a moment, he'd thought he was dreaming.

Memories hit him like a sixer. Harder than he'd hit the winning runs in the final over of the cricket match last week.

Yep, it was Lucy. He walked over to the fence line, and his horse ambled along behind him, munching the last tufts of grass around the fence posts. He stood there and watched her floating in the dam for a few minutes before he called out.

The small copse of trees where they'd both lost their virginity one warm winter afternoon still stood in the middle of the wheat paddock. For a few weeks afterwards, he'd expected to see her grandfather arriving with a shotgun because they'd used no protection. Condoms weren't something he'd carried when he'd been fencing back in those teenage years. He grinned; it had been a good lesson for a teenage boy.

Those lazy afternoons popped into his head when Lucy stood in the water and waded out towards him. Her one-piece swimsuit clung lovingly to her curves, and he let his gaze sweep her length. Her body was more womanly than when she'd been an athletic teenager.

And drop-dead gorgeous.

As he kissed her cheek and stepped back, he became the subject of her intense scrutiny. 'Just a quick visit.' Her voice was still low and husky, enough to send a shiver down his spine.

He shook his head. 'Thank you, but no, not at the moment. Your grandmother wouldn't be too impressed if I rolled into her kitchen.'

Lucy looked up curiously as she bent to pull on her boots.

'Nice look. Blundstone boots and swimmers. Takes me back a few years.' He chuckled at the picture she made.

Quirky, but still very, very beautiful.

A flush ran up her cheeks as she looked up at him. 'Why wouldn't Gran be happy about you coming over? You used to live in her kitchen when we were kids.'

Garth huffed a sigh and bit down on the regret that surfaced. 'It's a long story, Luce. You've been gone a long time. What is it? Six years?' He knew full well exactly how long it had been since she'd left but he wasn't going to let her know that. A man had to have his pride.

'Five,' she said.

'Well, I'm sure it won't be long till you catch up on everything that's happened while you've been gone.' His horse snickered, and he turned. 'I've got a crew waiting for me at the back paddock down near the bore, so I've got to go. Come on over to my place whenever you want.'

'Your place?'

'Yeah, the olds handed it over to me. Dad said there was no point waiting till they carked it. They've moved down to the South Coast. Got a beautiful house on the water at Jervis Bay.'

'That'll keep you busy.' She tipped her head to the side, and Garth caught his breath again. Lucy didn't look a day older than when they'd been at school. Her hair was still long, and her fringe brushed her high-arched dark eyebrows. Her lashes were wet from her swim, clumped together in long spikes. Yep, she was even more beautiful now.

'Got any kids yet to carry on the tradition?' she asked with a smile that showed off her pretty teeth.

'None that I'm aware of,' he said with a grin.

'And your wife? Does she work in town or help you out here?'

'My wife?' Garth fair snorted the words. 'What wife?'

'The girl from Narrabri you married. That wife.' Lucy stared up at him with her hands on her hips. She was such a petite little thing. But he knew better than to be taken in by the looks; Lucy Peterkin had a backbone of steel. Stubborn, just like her grandmother.

He shook his head and laughed.

'You got that one wrong. That was my cousin Brent. He got married just before Mum and Dad moved south. His wife's family has a big cotton property out near Moree, and he's looking after that.'

'So you're all settled here in the Pilliga?' Lucy's forehead wrinkled in a frown, and a feeling that he'd been judged and found wanting flickered through Garth.

'No desire to see the world?' she said.

'Oh, I'm not quite a cow cocky yet, Lucy. I've travelled.' His voice was clipped, but he tempered his words with a smile. 'Unlike some of us who grew up out here at Prickle Creek, I'm happy to stay.' He didn't mention his degree and his time working in Western Australia, saving as much money as he could, working in the mines. Dad thought he was mad, but even as the only child, Garth refused to be given the property; he'd worked his butt off as a mining engineer for three years and had paid for the beach house down on the coast for his parents before he'd let them sign over the farm. Lucy didn't need to know all that: she'd made her assumptions about him, and it hurt, so he changed the subject.

'Now what's all this crazy'—he put his hands in a square to his eye, mimicking her action —'that you are on about?'

'You've given me a fabulous idea, Garth. Can I come over to your place later and tell you about it?'

'Sure can. I'll expect you after dinner. Okay?' He tipped his hand to his hat. 'It's been good catching up, but I have to go. Just came up here to fix the fence.' He shook his head and couldn't help the grin that was tugging at his lips. 'Couldn't believe my eyes when little Lucy Peterkin strolled along the road. It's really good to see you again.'

Lucy reached for her dress hanging on the fence and pulled it over her head. 'Ditto. I'll see you later.' She looked at him from beneath lowered lids. 'That's if you're sure you want to have a city slicker come visit.'

With that parting shot, she turned and headed for the red dusty road winding around the paddock, where the wheat swayed in golden ripples as the afternoon breeze strengthened.

'See you soon, then.' Garth stood and watched her walk away before he turned to the waiting horse with a frown. If he didn't know better, he could have sworn she was flirting with him. He wasn't really happy with the interest that Lucy Peterkin sparked in him. Not the way things were at the moment, anyhow.

Garth was thoughtful as his horse cantered down to the back paddock. Maybe inviting her over hadn't been such a great idea.

CHAPTER 4

On Monday morning, Liam Smythe hefted his backpack onto his shoulder and stepped onto the footpath outside Sydney International Airport. Crowds of people rushed past him, in and out of the sliding doors; horns blared, and the car fumes hung in the air. He could have been in any city in the world. Travellers queued for taxis, purpose written on their faces, and for the first time in a long while, Liam realised he, too, had a purpose today. Out of habit, he patted his shirt pocket for a cigarette and sighed. He'd given it up, but the habit remained. Nor had he had one drink on the whole thirty-hour flight from London.

He tipped his head back and stared at the vivid blue sky. Even in the city, the sky was a brilliant blue. Nowhere else in the world was the sky this blue; he was looking forward to getting out west, where it was an even deeper hue.

To the big sky of the outback. The only place where he'd ever felt truly at home; he'd searched from Indonesia to the United States and kidded himself he'd been fairly settled in London for the past two years. He had been until—no, don't go there.

Liam glanced down at his watch. He'd taken an earlier flight and called Jemima from the transit lounge in Dubai, and she'd agreed to wait for him in Sydney so they could travel out to Prickle Creek Farm together.

'So what's the go?' he'd asked his sister on the phone.

'I don't know. I've got a horrid feeling that one of the olds is sick. That's the only reason I'm going back out there.'

'I was surprised you said yes. What about Lucy and Seb? Did they get the call too?'

'Lucy's already gone home but she said Seb won't go.'

'Not surprised. He and Gran had a huge ding-dong row after Mum's funeral. He said some pretty nasty stuff to her. Seb always held a grudge when we were kids, too.'

'And you were the perfect child? Give me a break, Liam. You and Seb were always vying to be the best at everything, and you always fought with him.'

It was true; the rivalry between them as kids had been strong, but those days of growing up at Prickle Creek had forged a bond between the

LUCY

four cousins. It was sad that life and tragedy had broken it; they were grown up now and all very different people. In one way, he hoped that Seb didn't come out to the farm; Liam could handle Jem and Lucy without getting his emotions all fired up, but one word from Seb—and he was the master of sarcastic comments—would bring him undone.

A taxi driver blared his horn in a continuous blast, and Liam stared at the line of cars picking up passengers. Had he really chucked his job at one of the top British newspapers and headed home after one phone call from his grandmother? Especially in the current job market where journalists were being retrenched all over Australia and the market for freelance work was drying up. After he'd had a break, he'd have to go back overseas. That's where he'd made his name, and that's where he'd have more chance. He must have had a bad hangover the night she called.

Jeez, he needed a break. He ran his hand through his short-cropped hair. The last couple of years had been tough. A quick visit home and he'd be off into the wide world again

His phone buzzed.

'Liam? Where are you?' He listened to the precise tones of his sister's voice. She'd worked hard to get the posh accent in place. She sounded more Sloane Ranger than half the Pommie girls he'd gone out with since he'd arrived in London.

'Yeah, I'm already out on the footpath where the drop-off and pick-up is. Where are you, pipsqueak?'

'Don't call me that,' Jemima said, irritation lacing her voice and Liam grinned. 'Wait there. I won't be long, just coming through the Eastern Distributor Tunnel now. We can get an early start and drive out all day Sunday.'

He grinned. Always the organiser.

'Sounds like a plan. See you, Jemmy.'

'Jemima.' Her voice was not amused. Liam's grin widened. He could still push her buttons. He waited on the edge of the footpath as instructed, waiting for his sister to arrive, and his eyes widened when a black Audi TT pulled up beside him. Jemima called through the window. 'Liam, over here.'

He shook his head as he hefted his bag into the back and climbed into the front seat. 'Hey, sis. Nice wheels. You must be doing okay.'

She didn't answer but blew an air kiss over to him as he closed the door. Glancing over her shoulder, she indicated and pulled out into the traffic. 'So are you okay to go west today? Don't need a sleep first?'

'I can sleep in the car on the way out.'

'Good. I figure the sooner we get out there, the sooner we can get back to the city.'

'Yeah. We're on the same wavelength there.' Liam nodded and gestured to the fancy dashboard of the Audi. 'Are you stopping somewhere to pick up another car, or are you going to really upset Gran and turn up in this?'

'This is my car, and this is what we are driving to Prickle Creek in. And this is what we will arrive in.' Jemima's face was set in a closed expression. 'She wants us out there so badly; she gets us on our terms.'

Liam shrugged and leaned his head back on the seat. 'Wake me up when we hit the first coffee stop out of the city. I'll need a hit of caffeine before I can share the driving.'

For the first time, Jemima's face cracked into a smile. 'Oh no, you don't, big brother. You're not getting your hands on this baby. I'll drive the whole way, thank you very much.'

CHAPTER 5

Lucy took heed of Garth's words and didn't mention to Gran that she was going to the McKenzie farm after dinner. Gran had answered Lucy's nonstop stream of questions over dinner, but she'd seemed preoccupied. After they had cleared the table, they worked together in the kitchen, making a few more batches of scones ready for the next day.

'Do you still make your blackberry Jam, Gran?'

'No. I haven't had anyone to pick the berries for me, Lucy. I'm too old to go climbing all over those bushes. They're out of control in the back paddocks. If you feel like going down to pick some while you're here, we could make some jam together.' The guilt that hit Lucy squarely in the chest got worse with Gran's next words.

'You get the thermos flasks from the pantry, Lucy. I just need to sit down for a while.' Lucy frowned when Gran put a hand to her chest and reached for a small bottle of tablets on the kitchen windowsill.

LUCY

'What's wrong?' Lucy closed the door of the walk-in pantry and followed her grandmother to the living room.

'Nothing.' Gran waved a dismissive hand. 'My digestion isn't what it used to be. Just a bit of heartburn.'

'Really? That's all?'

'Yes. That's all.' But Gran didn't meet her eye. 'Now go and get those flasks out and make sure we're set for the morning. It's going to be a busy day.'

'Okay, and then if you don't mind, I'm going to go for a bit of a drive around.'

'That's good. I'm happy you want to have a good look at the place. Have a look at the blackberries, but if you get out of the car, watch out for snakes. Your Pop said there've been some big eastern browns around since the heat arrived.'

'Ergh.' Lucy shivered.

Gran smiled, and her whole face softened. 'You never were one for the farm, were you, Lucy?' Although she smiled, her eyes were sad.

'That's not true. I loved spending time with you and Pop when we were kids.' The familiar lump of grief rose into her chest, and she hurried on before it turned to tears. 'Is the old bore still running? We used to have such fun out there.'

'I know that was the only way that your parents could get you out here after you started high school. Your mother would say—'

Their eyes met and held, and Gran looked away, but not before Lucy saw the sheen of tears in her eyes.

'Well, get going. It'll be dark before you get back.' Gran's voice was brisk, and when Lucy looked at her, there was no sign of tears in the faded blue eyes. Maybe she'd imagined it.

Although the old woman's hands held a faint tremble as she straightened the tea towel on the oven rail. 'Yes, a lot of the bores have been capped off, but your grandfather loves getting in that one. He says it helped his knee.' It was as though Mum hadn't been mentioned at all.

'Good, I'll drive out that way too. So his operation is tomorrow, Gran? How serious is it?'

'Yes, it's tomorrow. And then he'll be home a couple of days after that. I'll get you to drive me in to visit him on Wednesday night.' Gran's voice was a bit shaky, but she didn't answer Lucy's second question, and she let it go.

'We can all go and visit him tomorrow after the op. He'd love that, wouldn't he?'

LUCY

'That he would.' Gran yawned as Lucy picked up her car keys.

Lucy took a deep breath, walked over, and put her arms around Gran's shoulders, surprised by her frailty; she knew Gran hated any signs of affection. 'I won't be too long. I'll make you a cup of tea for supper when I get back if you're still awake.'

'Don't bother with that. I'll be asleep.' Gran stepped back and waved her hand. 'I'll see you in the morning. It's going to be a busy day.'

'Okay. Sleep well, Gran.'

Lucy pulled on a pair of old wellingtons that were in the boot room off the laundry before heading out to the big three-bay shed. She'd decided to take Pop's old farm ute. As expected, the keys were in it. It started with the rattle of the diesel engine, and Lucy engaged the clutch; it had been years since she'd last driven a manual car, but she soon got the hang of it again. Part of the attraction for the cousins in their early teens had been driving Pop's farm utes around the property. Lucy looked down at the worn leather and the chipped dashboard. She was sure this was one she'd driven in her early teens, about twenty years ago. Another deep breath and push away the memories. God, if she kept going back to the old days, she'd be a blubbering mess before the two weeks were up. Deep breath and chin up. Time to focus on persuading Garth to be a part of her campaign.

First off, Lucy headed the ute down towards the old bore and parked there for a while, watching the hot water spurting from the large round pipe. She stepped out of the ute, keeping an eye out for snakes; the water attracted them. The grass where they'd had their family picnics was long and unkempt, and a few pieces of rusty equipment lay around the paddock. She'd round Liam and Jemmy up over the weekend, and they'd all come down here and clean up. It was too nice a place to let go to rack and ruin.

She climbed back up into the ute and took the back road over towards the McKenzie farm; it was only a few minutes before she pulled up at the gate in the fence dividing the two properties. The gate didn't move as she pushed it open, and Lucy frowned as she spotted a huge shiny padlock, surprisingly securing it to the fence rather than the usual loop of steel that had previously circled the post. There was no way to get through it unless she had a key. She shrugged, got back into the ute, and headed past the homestead and onto the dirt road that passed the various properties. It was a few extra kilometres down to the main gate of the McKenzie farm, and she flicked the lights onto high beam, keeping an eye out for wild pigs and kangaroos. In the paddock on the other side of the road, a spotlight lit up the horizon as contract shooters hunted feral wildlife.

The wheels of the ute rattled as she drove over the cattle grate at the entrance to the McKenzie farm, and as she parked her car, three border collies and a red kelpie danced around the vehicle, yapping a welcome—or a warning.

Garth was sitting on the wide verandah, holding a beer. He stood and waited at the top of the steps as she climbed down, a little bit of shyness settling in her chest. Garth had surely grown into a fine-looking man, and the feelings she'd had for him as a teenager tugged at her memory as she stood there feeling a little bit awkward.

Don't be silly, she told herself.

Fresh and glowing with health, he'd obviously showered and changed from his dusty work clothes. Damp curls brushed the collar of his pale blue shirt. Garth had been her first real boyfriend, and she'd fallen pretty hard for him back in those hormonal teenage days. He'd been the only boy she'd ever been interested in at high school; one year ahead of her, he'd left the district after his final year, and she'd missed him. And he was still a looker; if anything, his looks had improved with maturity.

'Want to sit outside? It's a lovely night.' His deep voice washed over her as he held up his glass. 'A beer or a wine?'

'A beer would be great, thanks.' Lucy reached up and dabbed at the perspiration on her brow. 'It's going to take me a while to get used to this western heat again.'

A calico hammock swing filled with brightly-coloured cushions hung next to where Garth had been sitting, and she settled into it, tucking her feet beneath her. The verandah was enclosed with a light screen to keep the flies and bugs out, but Lucy could still see through the light gauze screen over the paddocks. Dark shapes dotted the lush grass, and the occasional muted call of a beast reached her as the cattle settled under the trees for the night. A background hum of cicadas filled the night air. She took a deep breath; no animal smells drifted across and the air was sharp with the smell of eucalyptus from the stand of white-barked trees behind the house.

LUCY

Lucy smiled when Garth handed her a glass of beer. 'Thanks, but out of the bottle would have been fine. I'm still a country girl.' She turned back to the paddock and pointed with her free hand as he sat down. 'So you're not harvesting yet?'

'No, we're about a week behind you over here.' She caught a white flash of teeth as he smiled in the semi-darkness. 'Besides, your grandfather has booked out every contractor in the district this week.'

'Tell me about it,' she said with a laugh. 'I've been helping Gran make sandwiches and scones most of the afternoon.'

Garth stared past her and his voice was serious. 'So tell me, how are they really?'

'Really, what?' Lucy sensed a hidden question beneath his words.

'Are they well? Coping okay? It's a lot of land for an elderly couple to look after.'

For some reason, Lucy wanted to spring to the defence of her grandparents, but she thought carefully before she spoke. The farm had looked tired and run down, but Liam and Seb, when Seb arrived—she knew he would give in—would spruce it up. 'Yes, it is, but they're going okay.

Once Pop's had his knee operation, he'll be as good as new and back on his horse.'

Garth nodded and didn't say anything, and Lucy spoke to fill the uncomfortable silence. 'So tell me, why is the back gate locked? The one at the back of the bore? I tried to take the shortcut, but there's a big padlock on the gate, so I had to come around the long way.'

Garth stared out over the paddocks and didn't answer for a moment. Lucy sensed he was trying to find the right words. 'The relationship between the two properties has changed a lot since my olds moved away.'

'In what way?'

'Your grandmother doesn't like the way I work. Newfangled ideas, she says, and I guess she didn't want the close relationship to continue when they left. The padlock went up on the gate after—'

He broke off, and Lucy prompted him to continue. 'After what?'

'No matter.' He waved his hand out towards the paddock. 'I'm happy with the way things are going. It's hard work by myself some days, but I'm making a go of it.'

'Pop said cattle prices are up.'

'Yes, they are. That sweetens the load a lot. But enough of farm stuff; I know how much you hated it when you were a kid. Tell me what you've been up to since you moved away.'

'I didn't hate it. There were some good parts.' Lucy took a deep breath, trying to forget about the great times they'd shared those last two years before Garth had left. 'I'm in advertising now. A potted version of my life for you: I did a degree in creative writing, and I fell into a dream job. I'm a freelance copywriter in Sydney, and I work out of one of the big firms. And maybe you remember how much I loved art? Caleb lets me do a lot of the graphics work, even though my degree is in writing, and he wanted me as a copywriter.'

'Freelance?'

'Yeah, I have a cubby hole at Goodbody and Grech for the work I do for them, but I also do some work from home for other agencies. The new way of the world. SOHO.'

'Soho? I thought Soho was in London.' Garth tipped his beer up and took a long drink, and she grinned.

'It is, but it means 'Small Office, Home Office'. I telecommute, that is, I work from home some days.' She grimaced as she thought of what she had ahead in the next two weeks. 'I've got a fair bit of work on at the moment and I thought I could work from here, but I think I'm going to be busy helping Gran with the contractors, and the internet connection is woeful over at Prickle Creek Farm. I'm going to have to go into town and use the library to send my work to Caleb if it doesn't improve.'

'I don't think your grandparents accepted the NBN offer.'

Lucy nodded and wrinkled her nose. 'I think so too. They've still got a dial-up modem. I haven't heard those connecting noises since I was a kid. They're not into technology at all. I've got my dongle, but the service isn't as good out here. A bit far from the tower, I guess.'

'Yes, it's just out of town. But listen, don't waste time driving into town I've got an NBN connection here. You're more than welcome to come over here and work whenever you need to.' Garth smiled at her. 'Even if I'm not here, make yourself at home.'

'Oh, thank you. That's really kind of you.' Being able to save the hundred kilometre-plus round trip to town would make a difference. She hadn't broached to Gran that she might have to leave her some days. The two weeks were looking busy; by the look of things, the days were going to be full. If what Garth had said was right and Pop had booked all the harvesting contractors in the district, she and Gran and Jemima would be cooking and feeding a crowd all day and night. Lucy frowned; she'd been prepared to work late at night if she had to, but maybe it wasn't going to work out. But she'd find a way; there was no way she was going to let this opportunity pass her by.

'Earth to Lucy-Lou.' Garth's deep voice, filled with humour, broke into her thoughts.

'Oh, sorry, I was planning my days—and nights—in my head.' She picked up the beer glass from the table beside the hammock and sipped at it, appreciating the cold, bitter liquid as it cooled her throat.

'So what was the bright idea you had this afternoon?' Garth put his fingers in a square like she had at the dam. Lucy stared at his hands. They were the hands of a worker, tanned with fine dark hair on the top, and calluses on his palm. Even when he'd been a teenager, Garth had been a worker, and she'd loved the feel of his hands on her skin.

Don't go there. Stay focused.

'Hmm. How do I put this? I need to convince you what a fabulous idea this is.' Lucy put her glass down and tipped her head to the side. 'Maybe I can be extra persuasive. Not just good for me, but good for you. It would be a well-paid job, so if you need extra money for the farm it might come in handy.'

'You always talked in riddles, Lucy-Lou. What would be a paid job?'

A shimmer of warmth ran through her at the affectionate nickname he'd always used for her.

'I'm about to develop a proposal for a new product campaign, and I need a man.' She giggled as her words ran together in her excitement. She'd given a lot of thought to the concept this afternoon as she had worked with Gran, weighing flour, cracking eggs, and mixing scone dough.

'You need a man?' There was a trace of humour in his tone as he waggled his eyebrows at her, and she played along.

'I do. A manly man, rugged, outdoorsy and strong.' She lifted her hands to form a frame. 'If only I'd had a camera with me this afternoon, I could have taken a great shot of you. You were hot and sweaty, but you looked so'—whoops, she wouldn't say sexy. Flirting was fun and harmless but she didn't want to give Garth the wrong idea. 'So Aussie and so hard working. A real bloke.' Her voice faltered as he stared at her, his eyes dark and intense.

'So what's this concept you've had? What's the product you need a man for?'

'Sexy lingerie. It's a huge Australian firm, and they're launching a new product.'

'Me?' Garth spluttered in his beer, and his eyes widened. 'And you want me to model underwear?'

'No, of course not, silly.' Lucy shook her head and laughed at the look of horror on his face. 'I need a backdrop for the models, and you, the big sky and the horse this afternoon were perfect. I've been looking at sophisticated city settings, and nothing has felt right.' She looked across at him. 'And you, Mr McKenzie, gave me a brilliant concept this afternoon. I'll tell Seb to bring all his camera gear when he comes.'

'Seb?'

'Yeah, Liam and Jemima are coming up to Prickle Creek Farm, and I'm pretty sure Seb will be too.' She jumped out of the hammock, walked across and crouched in front of his chair. 'So what do you think, Garth? Would you be interested in helping me out?'

'Hmm.' He leaned forward and held her gaze. 'Would it mean your visit would be a bit longer?'

'Possibly. I can work from here just as well as I can from my apartment.' Excitement flooded through her as the campaign formed in her head. 'I was meant to come out here! I've been thinking about this campaign for weeks, and inspiration has deserted me. This proposal can be the big break that launches my career. So what do you say?'

'Can I have some time to think about it?'

'You sure can. And I'll get some figures together for you. I'll get you the best rate I can.'

Garth looked down and she sensed he didn't want to talk about money. Maybe things were tight and that was why he was working here by himself.

Lucy pushed up to her feet. 'Thanks for the beer. I'd better get back and see what other jobs Gran has lined up for me.' Garth stood and held the screen door open for her and then followed her down to the driveway. She reached up and kissed his cheek. 'And think about my idea. It would be great to work together while I'm here.'

'I will.'

LUCY

As she leaned back, a warm hand reached around the back of her neck. 'For old times' sake.' Garth pulled her closer. Lucy closed her eyes as his lips lightly brushed across hers. It was a brief butterfly kiss. 'Something to make you want to stay around a bit longer, Lucy Lou.'

Lucy was thoughtful as she drove back to Prickle Creek Farm. The next couple of weeks were going to be busy . . . and interesting. Maybe she could ignore the prickles and the flies.

***

Garth sat on the verandah a long time after the tail lights of Lucy's granddad's ute had disappeared over the low rise in the far paddock as she headed for the road. It was crazy, but he'd hated Lucy leaving him tonight. He'd always enjoyed the time they'd spent together, and if he was honest, he'd never found another woman who had measured up to her. They'd had fun together, and it was a shame they'd both headed away from Prickle Creek to follow their dreams. For a while, Garth let his thoughts linger on the "what ifs".

Maybe if he hadn't left the district straight after school, their relationship might have developed. It hadn't been a hard break at the time. He'd been excited about heading out into the wide world, getting an education, and experiencing life away from Prickle Creek. Huh, if only he'd known then, that all he'd learned was that Prickle Creek was where he wanted to be. Lucy had already been planning to move to Sydney, anyway. Hell, she'd been talking about that since she'd hit her teens. Maybe he could have gone to uni in Sydney, and they could have stayed together.

Yeah, so he'd left and seen the world. He'd got his degree, and he'd landed a plum job at a gold mine in the wilds of Western Australia, which had earned him mega dollars in just three years. Enough money to buy a house on the coast for his parents. Enough money to come back and make a real go of the farm. He'd travelled enough to know that the Pilliga Scrub and the Mackenzie Farm were where he wanted to be. He loved living here, and he loved the work. He had friends in town when he wanted company. The experimental work he was doing with different types of wheat was interesting.

So why was he feeling so restless tonight?

What would have happened if Lucy hadn't gone away to the city? Would she have married another farmer and stayed here on the land? In the six months he'd been back, he'd been to a couple of the Bachelor and Spinster balls that were held in the large wool shed on the edge of town. It had caused a bit of a stir when he'd come back to the district, and there were plenty of local girls who had been keen to have a dance and have a drink—and more if he'd wanted.

Crazily, he'd always compared them to Lucy Peterkin, the girl he'd had a crush on all of high school. The girl who'd let him kiss her on her sixteenth birthday.

Then, after her eighteenth birthday…

He lifted his beer and stared over the paddocks in the direction of Prickle Creek Farm.

Lucy Peterkin. That's who was getting under his skin. But he wasn't going to let it burrow any deeper. She'd go back to the city.

And I'll be alone again.

Funny that she'd thought he was married with kids. It hadn't seemed to have bothered her at all.

Maybe it was time the farmer took a wife.

CHAPTER 6

Lucy rose at daybreak and called Sebastian as soon as it was a decent hour, full of glee that she could impart the news that Liam and Jemmy were on the way. It would be late afternoon before her cousins arrived, and the anticipation of being together again filled her with excitement. Gran was quiet as they buttered the scones and filled picnic baskets, and the food was ready when the first contractor appeared at the door just after nine o'clock.

'Woo hoo, what have we here? Some newly hired help, Mrs Peterkin?' The young man lifted the edge of the red checkered cloth, keeping the scones warm in the basket.

'Tommy Robinson, you get your hand away from those scones, and no, this is my granddaughter, Lucy.' She slapped his hand away from the basket as he peered in at the scones. Lucy smiled back at the appreciative grin that came her way when he raised his eyes.

'I think I'll volunteer for pick-up duty every day,' he said.

'Get away with you,' Gran said. 'The boys will be waiting for their cuppa.'

LUCY

'See you later, love.' With a wink directed at Lucy, Tommy picked up the three loaded boxes, balanced them on one arm, and then picked up the small esky with the other. He turned to Gran with a wide smile. 'You too, Mrs P. The boys are looking forward to this. You still take the prize for the best scones in the district.'

'Get away with you, boy. Flattery won't work on me. Now, there's butter and jam in that esky with the milk,' Gran said firmly as she pointed to the small blue cooler, but Lucy noticed the flush that tinged her cheeks.

The morning raced by as Gran and Lucy prepared enough sandwiches to feed an army. Ten loaves of bread had thawed overnight, and two huge slabs of corned beef had simmered on the stove. Gran pulled out her show-winning pickles. As they cleaned up the kitchen afterwards, Lucy reached up and wiped away the perspiration that trickled down her neck. The dishwasher was loaded and running, and they were washing up the pots and pans in the sink.

'There's no way you could have done this without help, Gran.'

'Why not? I've done it every other year since you all took off.' Her voice was dry, but there was an undercurrent of sadness that tugged at

Lucy's guilt. They chatted as Gran washed and Lucy wiped the dishes.

'I'm a bit tired. I might go and have a lie-down after we finish here.' Alarm spiked through Lucy; Gran had always been snarky about people who needed a daytime nap. 'The day is for work' she'd always said.

'Just the Anzac bickies and the thermoses for smoko this afternoon?' Lucy asked casually.

Gran nodded.

'I'll do that.'

'That would be good.' Lucy's guilt climbed higher. Not only was Pop unwell but there was something wrong with Gran; she was starting to think.

'I think it's time that you and Pop thought about hiring some more help, don't you?'

Gran pursed her lips but wouldn't be drawn into any conversation about the farm.

'I saw Garth McKenzie at the dam when I went for my swim yesterday.' Lucy flicked a glance across as Gran plunged her hands into the hot soapy water again.

'My goodness, that water's hot. Pass me a hand towel, Lucy.' By the time she'd wiped her hands, the strange look had left Gran's face, and Lucy wondered if she'd imagined it.

LUCY

'What was that McKenzie boy doing on our land?' Her tone was as hard as the words.

Lucy's head flew up. 'He was being friendly. Is there a problem there?' Lucy stared at her grandmother. 'And why is there a padlock on the back gate? I saw that last night.'

'Did you try to go over there?'

'I did, and I ended up going there the long way around. Garth and I were good mates when we were at school. You and the McKenzies were best of friends once. What's happened?'

Gran sighed and hung the towel on the hook back on the sink. 'Yes, we were. It all gets too hard sometimes. And yes, there is a problem, but I'm not going to discuss it with you. When the others are here, we'll have a meeting.'

'A meeting? That's a strange thing to call a family chat,' Lucy ventured.

'Pah! A family? We haven't been that since—I have business to discuss with you all, and we'll do it formally.'

Gran turned away and headed for the hall. 'Tommy'll be back for those sandwiches soon. Don't go giving him any encouragement.'

'No, Gran. I'll be a sour old battleaxe, too,' Lucy muttered under her breath. As much as she hated to admit it, Sebastian wasn't far wrong.

Gran had been hard and cold after her first welcoming greeting, and Lucy was beginning to feel like the hired help. Maybe coming out to Prickle Creek Farm hadn't been such a good idea.

***

Garth lifted the bottom of his T-shirt and tugged it over his head before he threw it onto the bale of hay next to the wall. Sweat ran down his face as he stared at the motor in front of him. The pump at the dam that fed the major irrigation sprayers had given up the ghost, and he couldn't spare the time to take it to town to get it fixed. He'd lifted the motor from the pump yesterday and sat it in the shed, thinking about the problem overnight. Now, he narrowed his eyes and stared at it, remembering the pumps at the mine. On a few of his night shifts there, he'd watched the mechanics repair the equipment, and he'd often pitched in and passed tools to them.

He leaned over and unscrewed the arm at the back of the pump. It was bent; a grunt of satisfaction puffed from his chest. As much as he'd resented the time away from the farm, both at uni and at the mine where he'd worked as an engineer, those years away had contributed to his skill set back here on the farm. The cattle raising and the wheat growing were something he'd learned from Dad, but the education and the skills he'd picked up out in the world of work had made the time away worthwhile. He took the arm over to the workbench and hammered it until it was flat. He lifted it up, checked it was no longer bent, and walked back over to the motor. Leaning over, he carefully screwed it back onto the pump. Garth pulled the starter cord and grinned when the motor fired first time.

Damn, if only everything was that easy. Satisfaction flowed through him for a job well done. Solving little problems like that showed to him every day how much he loved being out here on the Mackenzie Farm. He'd never told his parents, but the number of times he'd almost pulled out of uni and quit his job to come back home had been more frequent than he admitted.

But it was all worthwhile. In the last six months since he'd arrived back home, he'd bought out his parents—the farm was his—and had a new farmhouse built. Cattle prices were high, this year's wheat harvest promised to be the best yet, and he was building the farm up into one of the best properties in the district. Never again would he have to leave the Pilliga Scrub and go back to working for someone else.

What was that Lee Kernaghan song he'd cheered himself up with in Western Australia when he didn't think he could stand being away from home anymore? *A country boy.* He hummed as he put the tools away.

'Way out here is where I ever want to be, thank God I'm a country boy.'

CHAPTER 7

'Damnation, bloody hell and bollocks.' Sebastian muttered under his breath as he threw a couple of pairs of jeans and spare T-shirts into an overnight bag on the Monday after Lucy had left. 'Two days and that's it.'

He'd go for two days and see what the old bat wanted. When Lucy had rung and told him she was going to town to buy him a hat, he knew exactly what she meant. Liam was going to Prickle Creek Farm.

'You are kidding me, right?'

'Nope.' Lucy's voice was smug. 'Liam has landed, and he and Jemmy are on the way here now. They'll be here tonight. It's Sunday, Seb. You could get on your bike and be out here by dark, too.'

'Aw no, Luce. I don't want to.'

'You sound like the whining three-year-old you used to be.' Then, her voice was serious. 'Come on, Seb. Gran's not well. I've been watching her, but she won't tell me anything. So get yourself on your bike and get out here.'

'All right.' Sebastian knew he was being difficult but damn it, he'd rather step into a nest of vipers than front his grandmother.

'And Seb?' This time, Lucy's voice had a wheedling tone.

'What else?' Seb ran his hand through his hair.

'Bring your gear with you. I have a small job for you.'

'Goes without saying, I would have brought it anyway. And Lucy? Two days, and then I'm outta there. *Capiche*?'

'*Capiche*. Love ya, boy.' Lucy's laugh tinkled down the phone. 'Can't wait to see you. What paddock are you going to do the nudie run in?'

'Bugger off, Luce.' He disconnected and zipped up his bag, but a grin hovered around his lips. Even though the old bat would be a pain, he was looking forward to catching up with his cousins.

Three hours later, Sebastian was on his BMW, and the thrill of the speed and the wind whistling past his face soothed his mood a little. His trepidation about going back to the farm for the first time since the funeral dissipated as his powerful bike flew along the highway. He turned off the new Hunter Express bypass and onto the Golden Highway, and soon, the green paddocks of the horse studs of the upper Hunter Valley were flashing by. Peace and serenity filled him.

Of the four cousins, he was the one who loved the land, but there was no way he'd ever let his grandmother know that. Pop always welcomed him home, but his grandmother had always been judgmental, and nothing he'd done had ever measured up to bloody Liam. Sebastian missed the country; there was nothing like the colours of the paddocks and the big sky out west. Even the thought of the red dust and the prickles of the Pilliga Scrub enticed him. He grinned beneath his helmet as he leaned into a sweeping curve. To his friends, Sebastian was the consummate metrosexual of the trendy crowd; they didn't know the country boy who lurked beneath his city exterior.

A city boy through and through. In his signature black turtlenecks and with his long ponytail, he'd roamed the bars with his camera snapping the in-crowd for the social pages until Lucy got him a start at her agency.

And he hated every minute of his city life.

No one knew that except for his grandmother, the old crow.

##

Halfway through their journey, Jemima relented and let Liam drive her beloved sports car. When he'd woken up as she'd turned onto the Golden Highway, his sister had been on for a chat, and they'd talked nonstop as they headed for Dubbo.

'So you're doing okay?' He gestured to the car.

'Yes, I'm doing very well. I've bought myself a unit at Mosman, too.'

'Oh la de da,' Liam retorted with a laugh.

After a coffee break at Dunedoo, he took over the driving and Jemima relaxed with her feet stretched out. 'So what are your plans, bro? I was surprised that you came home to the royal summons.'

'Gran needs us all.'

'What do you think is wrong?'

'She'll tell us when she's good and ready, but not until we're all there.'

'The Famous Four, hey? Back together again.' Jemima's voice was soft as she stared through the window. 'We used to have great holidays out at Prickle Creek Farm with Gran and Pop, didn't we?'

'We did.' They'd built forts, swum in the dam and mustered cattle with the quad runners. They'd all felt grown up when they were allowed to go down to the hot bore at night and lie back and look at the stars as they scared each other silly with stories.

'Remember the Pilliga Princess story?' Jemima shot him a grin.

'I was just thinking about that. The Aboriginal ghost lady who always wore a fishing hat. The truckies were so scared of her they wouldn't stop for a kip anywhere on the Pilliga Road. I haven't thought of that story in years.'

'Poor Seb, you were so mean to him. 'I'll never forget that night he ran all the way back to the farmhouse, and Gran whopped his behind for not staying with us.'

'I did wind him up, didn't I?' Liam stared at the straight road ahead. He and Seb had never had an easy relationship. 'You know, I haven't seen him since the funeral. Have you?'

'I've run into him a couple of times at pubs in the city. But not for a couple of years now. He's a top-flight photographer now, you know. Very well respected.'

'I know.' Liam shook his head. 'I'm not that bad. I've kept up with the family, even if I have to Google you all to see what you're up to.'

'The accident really changed our lives, didn't it? I think of everything as before and after.'

'Me too.' Liam shifted back a gear as they came up behind a cattle truck, and the smell of cattle seeped through the vents. 'Screwed us all up big time. Have you heard from Dad lately?'

'No, not since he was in South America.'

They were quiet for a while as Liam concentrated on the road, each lost in their thoughts.

Jemima took in a deep breath. 'Ah, the smell of the country. As much as I hate to admit it, I have missed it, you know.'

'Have you been out here lately?'

'No.' She shook her head. 'This is the first time since the funeral, and I'm a bit nervous.'

''Don't worry, you're not Robinson Crusoe.'

##

Three hours later, Jemima cursed and fought for control as the Audi slipped from left to right on the wet road. A light shower of rain had turned the six-kilometre stretch of dirt road between the main Coonamble Road and Prickle

Creek Farm into a slippery track. It took them over half an hour to get to the gate of the property, and when the red and green sign appeared on the fence, she pulled over. 'I'd forgotten how far down the road the farm was. But you know what? It still all looks the same.'

'It does. I feel about eighteen again. Prickle Creek Farm,' Liam read the words on the sign before he turned to his sister. 'Why did you stop?'

'Because I need confidence and war paint.'

He huffed an impatient sigh when she reached for the makeup bag on the floor of the back seat and proceeded to lather stuff on her face before brushing her hair. She finished off with bright red lipstick and a puff of strong perfume.

'Gawd, Jemmy. I'll stink too. Give it a break.'

'Jemima, and it's Chanel No 5.' She looked at him through heavily mascaraed eyelashes.

Liam shook his head. 'Do women really think that stuff makes a man look twice?'

'Oh, button it, Liam.' Jemima took a deep breath. 'I can hide behind it, Jemima Smythe, aloof model who doesn't do emotion.'

Liam grinned at her. 'Well, if you did, I think your face would crack with all that gunk on it.'

For that, he copped a punch on his upper arm.

'And don't you even think about saying a word of that to Gran or Lucy,' Jemima said.

'Don't worry, Jem. We're all in this together. Solidarity. Okay?' Liam knew she was as nervous as he was about coming home. It had him beat how they had all jumped to Gran's summons. Maybe it was because she'd never asked them for anything before. They both turned their heads as a black motorbike whizzed around the car, its rider crouched low over the machine.

'Sebastian, if I am correct.' Jemima started the car, and they were both quiet as they followed the motorbike past the golden wheat paddocks that flanked the long drive to the farmhouse.

CHAPTER 8

Ralph stirred in his basket, and the outside dogs barked on the dirt driveway past the fence dividing the dusty drive from the lawn and Gran's colourful cottage garden. Lucy jumped to her feet. She and Gran had been watching the five o'clock news together in the lounge, both tired after a big day of preparing meals and cleaning up. Gran had nodded off despite her long afternoon nap, and Lucy had watched her as she dozed. The lines around her mouth were deeper, and there were dark shadows beneath her eyes. Tommy had collected the homemade beef pies and large saucepans of mash and peas before they sat down to watch the television for a much-needed break. The last round of sandwiches and fruit for the harvesters' late supper was packed up and ready to be collected. All they had left for the day was to fill the coffee flasks that would keep the night shift going as they cut hay all night.

'Someone's here.' Lucy crossed to the window and glanced over at Gran. The elderly woman held herself still as she lifted a handkerchief to her mouth before pulling herself to her feet. She strode to the kitchen ahead of Lucy.

'Fool boy's parked his motorbike on my lawn,' she muttered, and Lucy took a deep breath, feeling a measure of responsibility for talking Seb into coming. A low-slung black sports car, splattered with red mud, pulled up near the gate. As Lucy watched, Jemima uncoiled herself gracefully from the driver's seat and, despite the dusk light, dropped a huge pair of sunglasses over her eyes. A rush of emotion flooded Lucy as Liam opened the passenger door and stepped out of the car. She flew down the steps and launched herself at him. 'Liam,' she choked out.

'Luce!' He picked her up and swung her around before enfolding her in a bear hug. 'God, I've missed you, bub.'

Lucy's eyes were wet with happy tears. She and Liam had always been the pair to lead the two younger cousins into trouble. Jemima walked around the back of the car, and Lucy was engulfed in a cloud of expensive perfume as Jemima blew a couple of air kisses in her direction.

'Good to see you, Lucy.' She pointed a languid finger to the car. 'Liam, see to my bags, will you?' She stepped back as one of the kelpies brushed past her. 'Ergh. Look out, dog.'

Lucy looked over her shoulder. Seb was sitting on his bike, his helmet still covering his face. Gran was standing at the top of the steps, and Lucy's eyes pricked with tears as she saw Gran's knuckles, white and tense, where she gripped the railing.

I'm always the peacemaker. She walked over to Seb and took his arm as he stepped off the bike.

'Come on, I'll help you get through this,' she whispered. 'You can do it. I've survived twenty-four hours.' She nodded to Liam and Jemima. 'There's safety in numbers.'

An hour later, despite the huge food preparation day, Gran had rustled up the obligatory Sunday night baked dinner. The conversation around the dinner table had been polite, if stilted. The boys stacked the dishwasher while Gran took a shower, and Jemima and Lucy sat together out on the verandah. The only light in the solid darkness of the night was the distant headlights of the headers moving up and down the paddocks. The bug zapper hissed and spat as suicidal insects threw themselves at the purple light.

'So I guess it's the old room share.' Jemima lifted her glass of iced water and sipped, and Lucy noticed that her hand was shaking a little. She wasn't as calm as she was making out. 'You and me, Lucy.'

'Yeah. I guess.' Lucy looked over at her cousin. Her hair was immaculate, her nails painted a deep fire-engine red, and her lipstick appeared untouched despite the meal. 'You okay, Jemmy?'

'I go by Jemima these days.'

'Okay, then. Are you alright, Jemima?'

A sigh answered her, and Jemima put her glass down on the old scratched coffee table between the chairs. Gran had asked them to wait out here until she'd showered and would begin the family 'meeting'.

'Yes and no. I hate the tension between everyone, and I'm worried about what Gran is going to tell us. But I still can't believe we all dropped everything and rushed out here.'

'Family holds together no matter what happens, and I guess we're all worried about Pop,' Lucy said. 'He's always been such a strong, strapping man. I guess we thought he'd live forever.'

LUCY

'And Gran, too. She sounded so shaky on the phone, and I got such a shock. She's aged so much. What can be so important that we all had to be here while Pop is still in the hospital?'

Lucy shrugged as Liam and Seb walked onto the verandah. 'I guess we're going to find out soon. I have a feeling that it's not good news, though.'

The two men pulled up a chair each, and the silence was thick. Liam's jaw was set, and Seb stared out into the dark. Lucy couldn't stand it a moment longer. 'For goodness' sake, you pair. Would you stop circling each other like a pair of roosters? It's awful.'

'Still the peacemaker, Luce?' Liam glanced over at Seb and held his hand out. 'I guess that's the first time we've ever done the dishes here without having a blue, hey, coz?'

'Hard to blue without talking to each other.' Seb looked at him steadily before he took the proffered hand, and they shook.

'That's much better,' Lucy said. 'Now be friendly. We're all in this together.'

'Whatever this is,' Jemima muttered.

'So how's London?' Seb turned to Liam.

'Cold, noisy, busy.' Liam leaned back on the sofa beside Lucy. 'It's nice to be out here in the quiet.'

'What about you, Seb? Life treating you well?' Lucy looked at him; Liam obviously wasn't going to share that he'd kept tabs on all of them.

'I'm doing okay.' Seb shrugged and looked out at the paddocks again. Sadness lodged in Lucy's chest. Where was the happy camaraderie they'd all shared as they grew up? How could they get that back again? Was it too late given what had happened, and now that they all had their own lives? If this was what being an adult was like, she didn't like it at all. Suddenly, an unbidden image of Garth McKenzie filled her thoughts, and she let the warm feeling settle. Thinking about Garth made her feel much better.

They sat there quietly as they waited for Gran to appear.

Finally, Lucy couldn't stand the heavy silence any longer. Even Liam wasn't talking to her. 'I'm going to check on Gran; she's been an awfully long time.'

She walked along the hall towards the bedrooms just as Gran closed her bedroom door and stepped into the hall. Lucy was hit with a waft of Lily of the Valley talcum powder, and nostalgia flooded through her. She and Jemmy had always been allowed to borrow Gran's talc when they were little girls. Gran caught her eye as she held her floral brunch coat tightly across her thin chest, but her mouth was set, and she was very pale.

'Are you right, Gran?' Lucy took her arm and noticed how cold her skin was. 'You're not sick, are you?'

'No. I'm fine. Just a bit het up.'

That was a big admission from Gran, and Lucy held her arm as they walked out to the back verandah. She smiled when the boys stood until Gran sat down. They might be a pair of tough guys, but they remembered the manners that had been drilled into them all.

Liam sat back down and leaned forward with his hands dangling between his knees. Seb leaned back and kept his gaze on the now-dark paddocks. Jemima folded her hands in her lap as Lucy sat beside Gran. The silence was broken only by the distant sound of the headers in the far paddocks until Lucy cleared her throat.

'So, looks like we're all here and ready to listen, Gran.' Lucy kept her tone bright to cover the trepidation gripping her chest. Was one of the grandparents ill? Were they in financial trouble? A dozen scenarios flashed through her head as Gran cleared her throat.

'Thank you all for coming out. I appreciate it.' She nodded to Liam. 'Especially you, Liam, halfway across the world.'

Lucy ignored Seb's muffled snort as Liam held Gran's eye. He was the eldest grandchild, and he and Gran had always been close.

'We've not done well as a family. Tragedy dragged us apart, and we all dealt with it in our own ways. Losing our three girls'—Gran's voice was strong without a flicker of emotion—'almost destroyed Harry and me, but we've been remiss in letting you four go your own ways and losing touch with the land.'

She held up a hand before any of them could speak. 'Oh, I know you've made your own lives, and you are all doing well, but it's time to decide what the future holds.' Drawing herself up in the chair, Gran straightened her shoulders as she looked from one to the other. 'This property has been in our family for one hundred and fifty years, and the thought of it not being handed down to family is breaking your grandfather's heart. And mine, but if that is the way it has to be, so be it.'

'Gran.'

Again, she held up a hand as Liam and Lucy both tried to interrupt. 'Wait, you'll all have your turn to speak in a moment.'

Taking a deep breath, she looked past them. 'While your grandfather is in hospital, I want a decision made. So, when he comes home, it is a done deal. He doesn't need to know that I started it. As far as he knows, it is going to be your idea, Liam.'

Seb caught Lucy's eye, and his face was set. 'Okay, Gran. Cut to the chase. What do you want from us?'

Surprisingly, her eyes were warm as she turned to Seb, the youngest of the four. 'I want to know how strongly you feel about the future of Prickle Creek Farm. How much connection each of you has to our family land. Oh, I know it's been five years since any of you have been out here, but it's time to put that aside. We'll always grieve for your mothers, but it's time for the healing to begin. You're the generation to make the decision. You four are the future of Prickle Creek Farm.' Her eyes were clear and bright, and her voice was brisk.

Lucy was filled with admiration for her. Gran was one strong woman. 'What decision,

Gran?' She couldn't help the worry creeping into her voice.

Their grandmother turned to look at each of them in turn. 'I want to hear what each of you would have to say if I said I had an offer for the farm.'

A cold feeling ran through Lucy's chest. 'You're going to sell it?' she said with a frown.

'No!' Seb jumped to his feet. 'You can't sell.'

Lucy didn't miss the fleeting smile that crossed Gran's face as she looked at Seb and then turned to Liam. 'Liam?'

Liam dropped his gaze to the floor, and Lucy waited with bated breath until he lifted his head. 'I'd hate to see the farm leave our family.'

A quick nod from Gran as she turned to Jemima. 'Jemmy, what do you say?'

'No. You can't sell it.' Jemima's face was set in a stubborn frown as she folded her arms.

Finally, Gran turned to Lucy. 'You probably need to know it's Garth McKenzie who's offered to buy it.'

Lucy's mouth dropped open. Now she knew why Garth wouldn't come over here for a visit. He wanted to buy the farm. She didn't know how she felt about that. Knowing the Garth of old, surely it would be to help them out, but now, she wasn't so sure. A lot of time had passed since then, and now, as a landowner himself, maybe he wanted to expand his own property. The fact that he hadn't mentioned it last night made her cross.

Gran's face was set as she stared at Lucy. 'So Lucy? What say you?'

Confusion filled her, and she shook her head. 'Honestly? I don't know.'

Her grandmother's face creased in disappointment, and Lucy rushed on. 'I do know I would hate to see the property go out of the family. You're right, it would break Pop's heart, but I'm being realistic here. If you do keep it, how are you both going to look after it?'

Gran smiled and stood. 'I've heard what I wanted to hear. Now, I want you all to consider something, and you don't need me around to do it. Harry and I have discussed this, and if you are all willing to agree, we'll sign the property over to the four of you—equally—in one year's time.

'But there are conditions attached. For the next year, each of you will spend at least three months living here, learning the ropes and working the farm. If you're not prepared to do that—all of you working together and agreeing to the plan—as much as the idea sticks in my throat, we'll take up McKenzie's offer.' She smoothed her hands down her sides and turned to the door. 'I'll bid you all goodnight and see you in the morning. Bright and early, please; there's work to be done.'

Gran's back was ramrod straight as she headed down the hall.

A stunned silence was all she left behind.

LUCY

CHAPTER 9

It was Jemima's idea for them to head to the hot bore down at the back of the property. They grabbed their swimmers, and Liam pulled a six-pack of beer from the fridge. As Seb drove the old farm truck down the dirt road and turned into the back paddock, they were quiet, each lost in their thoughts. Lucy stared through the window as the lights of the McKenzie property glowed in the distance.

By omission, Garth had been dishonest with her. He should have been upfront and told her that he wanted to buy the farm. She wouldn't have thought badly of him. He was a kind man and was probably only trying to help. But he had lied to her, too. He'd said that Gran disagreed with his new-fangled ways.

The muted sound of the headers in the front paddock was overlaid by the rushing of the hot water from the pipe into the gravel-based bore. Jemima and Lucy slipped behind the trees and pulled their swimmers on. By the time they walked across to the hot pool, Seb and Liam were up to their waists, each holding a can of beer above the steaming water.

Lucy slipped into the hot water and floated on her back, looking up at the stars. This had always been her favourite place in the whole world. At night, the flies and dust and prickles could be put aside, and the cattle didn't come down here past the wheat paddocks. The night Mum and the aunties had been killed, Lucy had walked down here by herself in a daze of grief. She'd slipped into the bore, fully clothed, and let the peace of the night soothe her grief.

As much as it could, anyway. After a while, Liam, Jemima, and Sebastian appeared, and the tears that they had shared that night forged a bond that no distance could destroy.

The sky was velvet black, pinpointed with a million pricks of starlight. In the city, you don't see the sky like that at night. Peace descended on her, and the worry of the proposal she hadn't worked on receded even further to the back of her mind.

'So, what do we do?' Seb's voice was deep and echoed across the large expanse of water. 'She's really hit us with it, hasn't she?'

'What do you want to do?' Liam's lazy voice filled the night. 'You were the first one to come out with the resounding no, so you must feel strongly about it.'

LUCY

'I do,' Seb said. 'But I don't know if I want to put my life on hold to make it happen. What about the rest of you?'

The water rippled as Liam sank into the water and tipped his head back, one arm still holding his beer aloft. His dark eyes were shadowed in the starlight, and once again, Lucy picked up a sense that all was not well in his world.

But it was Jemima's voice that brought the most surprise. 'I'm in. I can take three months off and come out here. We can't let Gran sell.'

Liam turned to Seb. 'And if you want to make it happen so much, boyo, your life *is* going to have to be put on hold.'

'Lucy?' Seb's voice interrupted the panic that was building in her chest. It wasn't fair that this decision couldn't rest on her alone.

She bit her lip as she stared at the three faces looking at her, waiting for her to answer. She shook her head to clear the confusion and thought about what it would be like not to have Prickle Creek Farm as the one steady rock in her life.

'Okay, I guess so,' she said, slowly expelling her breath. But how could she make a decision like that when she wasn't sure? They all needed to think this through much more. 'But what happens then? We all spend three months here? Who looks after the place when we go back to our lives? If we have to sell, it might as well happen now. Let Gran and Pop enjoy the money. They can retire and have an easy life: travel, go on cruises and everything.' She knew she was babbling. 'Garth would be an ideal purchaser for the farm.'

'Still got a soft spot for McKenzie, have you, Luce?'

She almost saw red as Liam's words reached her. 'How dare you, Liam? No, I've only seen him once in the last seven years, and that was yesterday.'

'So you already knew about his offer?' Liam's tone was hard, and his face looked ghoulish as he stared at her from the shadows. He stood up and took a deep swig from the beer bottle.

'No, I didn't.' Her voice quivered; she was on the verge of tears. It was so unfair of Gran to put this on them with no warning. 'And *you* haven't said what you think yet, anyway, Liam. Your job's overseas. How are you going to spend three months here?'

'Leave her be, Liam. You're being mean.' Jemima's voice was quiet. 'We have to support each other. It's going to mean some huge changes for all of us if we take this on.' She turned to Lucy. 'Can you get time off work?'

'I'm freelance. As long as I get to Sydney once a month for the meeting, I can work from anywhere.'

All was quiet apart from the hot water splashing from the wide pipe into the bore as they were each lost in their thoughts. A fat yellow moon hung low above the tree line, and a white tawny frogmouth hooted as it flew over the bore. Lucy lay back in the steaming water and looked up at the stars. What did she really want to do? Could she live out here for three months to keep Prickle Creek Farm in the family? And what if none of them wanted to stay?

What would Garth think about it? Would he see her as a traitor? Why did he want to buy it, and more to the point, where would he get the money?

And where would Gran and Pop go? Her talk about cruises and holidays had been just that: an attempt to find a way to get out of leaving her life in Sydney and having to come back here. Mum's face came into her thoughts. Prickle Creek Farm was the one place where she had solid memories of Mum and her two sisters—her aunts in happier times.

Family holidays, Christmas, and many weekends were spent out here with the whole family: the three sisters and their husbands, Gran and Pop, and her three cousins. The three Bellamy sisters had stayed in Prickle Creek after they had married local men. Along with her Smythe and Richards cousins, Lucy had attended the town schools and had been inseparable as they'd grown up together.

Why had they let the accident drive them apart so easily? Why hadn't they leaned on each other? Seb was the only one she saw these days. Lucy lowered her feet to the gravel bottom of the bore and looked at each of them in turn. Jemima's makeup had washed off, and she looked like the Jemmy of old. Her cat-like eyes reflected the moonlight as she caught Lucy's eye and smiled. A real smile from the heart.

Sebastian was staring up at the sky, and his mouth was set in a straight line. Lucy knew him so well, and she could sense his confusion from the expression in his eyes. He was the youngest of the four, and he'd always been the one whose feelings were easy to read. He was the softest, and they had always babied him.

Liam's eyes were hooded, and he stared back at her as she looked at him.

'I'm in. I quit my job to come home, and I can work freelance from here for three months, too,' he said, holding her gaze steadily. 'What about you, Lucy? Are you in or not?'

She tilted her chin defiantly and nodded. 'I'm in.' Even as she agreed, dread rushed through her. It had been bad enough thinking of spending two weeks out here; how the hell would she cope with three months?

Two hours later, they still sat on the grass beside the bore, planning and tossing ideas back and forth. Liam had pulled an old tarp from the back of the farm truck and spread it on the grass to cover the cats eye prickles. The night was still and warm, and a slight mist hovered over the water.

'That's a great idea, Jemmy.' Seb's voice had become more animated the more they worked out a way to make this work.

Jemima ignored the old name and continued with her idea. 'If we do it in pairs over two stints, we'll be here to support each other, and it will be much easier. Three months on, three months off.

Gran should be happy with that; she gets each of us for six months instead of the three she stipulated.'

Lucy nodded. If there were two of them here at once, it *would* be easier to deal with things. 'What about Pop? I wonder why she asked us without him here.'

Seb scowled. 'Knowing Gran, I'd say Pop really doesn't know anything about this. Remember what she said? He has to think this is our idea.'

'He'll hate it,' Lucy protested. 'Gran can't make a decision like that without his input.'

'She would.' Liam nodded. 'As much as I love the old stick, she certainly wears the pants in the family.'

'She's worried about Pop,' Jemmy said.

Lucy stood and put her hands on her hips as the trees rustled above. A slight breeze had come up, but it was still hot, and perspiration ran down her back. 'So who's first?' she asked. 'And then once we've done the twelve months, what happens then? What do we do when the property is signed over? Do any of you really want to live back out here where we grew up? Come on, total honesty, guys.'

'Cross your heart and spit to death type honesty, Luce?' Liam's smile flashed. 'Okay, if we're being honest, I could settle back out here and work the place. Jemima?' He turned to his sister.

'Possibly.' She, in turn, looked at Seb. 'Sebastian?'

His emphatic nod didn't surprise Lucy at all. She was the odd one out. She was the city slicker, and she always had been. There were good memories out here, but too many sad ones. She honestly didn't know if she could do it—but it looked like she had to.

She'd give it her best shot. For Gran and Pop.

Lucy looked up and caught Seb looking at her, and a slow smile spread across her face. 'Now would be as good a time as any, Seb.'

He looked at her, and his brow wrinkled. 'What for?'

Lucy couldn't help the giggle that bubbled up out of her chest. Being home was feeling good. Now that they'd gotten Gran's news out of the way. 'You made me a bet, remember?'

Jemima and Liam looked at with interest as Seb spluttered. 'No, I don't remember any bet.'

Lucy turned to Liam. 'Seb said he wouldn't come home unless you did.' She stood straight in the water and watched the moonlight ripple on the small waves. 'And you did, so Seb, you lost.'

'No way.' His expression was mutinous, and Lucy's giggle turned into a laugh. 'Gonna renege, are you?'

'What was the bet?' Jemima asked, getting into the spirit of the teasing.

Lucy put her finger to her lips and said slowly, 'Now let me get this exactly right. What our dear cousin said was he would eat his hat and run around the paddock stark bollocky naked if Liam came home.'

Their laughter carried across the paddock and drifted into the night.

The cousins had come home to Prickle Creek, and they would make it work

They had to.

LUCY

CHAPTER 10

When Liam drove Pop's Toyota Lexus wagon into Prickle Creek on Wednesday afternoon, Sebastian opted to follow on his bike. Gran sat up straight in the front with Liam; Jemima and Lucy sat in the back as they headed into town to the hospital. The streets were so quiet compared to Sydney. Lucy pushed back the cold feeling that took hold of her every time she thought of staying here. At least it was keeping her cool in this relentless heat.

'Look.' Jemima's voice interrupted her brooding. 'The old milk bar still has the same tables and chairs outside as it did when we were in high school.'

'And the same owner,' Gran said drily. 'Not much changes in Prickle Creek, and that's not such a bad thing.' She flicked a glance over her shoulder at Lucy.

Gran's reaction to their acceptance of her deal had been low-key: a brisk nod followed by a hurry up to Jemima and Lucy to get the flasks filled for the contractors' supper. The harvest was half done, and a few of the workers had begun to move on to the McKenzie property. All had been quiet over there, and Lucy hadn't called Garth as she'd promised when she'd left the other night. Her head had been too full of the happenings at Prickle Creek Farm to think about her campaign proposal but she'd have to get moving on it soon. The plan was to go back to Sydney next week for her monthly meeting, present the proposal, and then come back and do the first of her three-month stints on the farm with Liam.

Unless there was a way she could get out of it.

And she wasn't quite ready to talk to Garth just yet. Lucy wanted to have the right questions ready for him when they finally met up. Between baking endless scones and biscuits, making sandwiches, and then trying to work on her proposal at night in the room she was now sharing with Jemima, there was no time to think about anything.

Liam parked the car, and the two girls waited as he helped Gran out. Sebastian roared into the car park, earning a dirty look from Gran.

'Honestly, he tries to wind her up on purpose,' Jemima whispered. Liam looped his arm through Gran's and led her into the hospital, followed by the rest of them.

LUCY

'Lucy!' As they walked through the foyer, Lucy turned around, and Gran's back stiffened as Garth walked across the polished floor towards them.

'Have you been in with Harry, Garth McKenzie?' Her voice was cold, and Sebastian and Liam flanked her as one.

'Yes, I visited Harry.' Garth smiled at Gran, but it wasn't returned. 'He seems to be doing well. He's looking forward to going home.'

'Come on.' Gran turned her back and walked away with the boys. Lucy's cheeks heated. There was no need for rudeness. She nudged Jemima. 'Tell Pop I'll be there in a minute.'

She stared at Garth and resisted the urge to fan her face as the heat moved up into her cheeks. She felt partly embarrassed at Gran's rudeness and partly due to the fluttering nerves that kicked into gear when he smiled down at her.

'Hello, Garth. Sorry I haven't called. I did mean to, but we've been really busy at the farm.'

'So it appears.' His eyes narrowed as he watched Gran and the three cousins walk down the long hall to the wards.

This time, it was Lucy's voice that was cold. 'So what's that supposed to mean?'

Garth shrugged. 'I didn't mean anything, just agreeing. Turn of phrase so to speak.'

'I think it's time we had a bit of a talk.' Lucy crossed her arms and stuck her chin out.

'About the photos you want to take?' he asked.

'Not just yet. And some other things I want to sort out.' In for a penny, she thought. 'Gran said you want to buy Prickle Creek Farm.'

'That's right. I made them an offer.'

Before she could help herself, Lucy burst out, 'And just where would you find the money for that, Garth McKenzie?'

Garth reached over and took her arm. 'Keep your voice down.' A few of the locals glanced at them from the waiting room. 'Go and see your granddad, and then we'll have a coffee in town.'

Lucy put her hands on her hips. 'Oh, will we just, Mr Bossy!'

'Do you want your questions answered, Lucy? I'm more than willing to have a chat.' His voice was patient.

'I don't have my car here. I'm travelling home with the family.'

'I'll wait until you finish your visit, and then I'll drop you home after we have a coffee and our chat.'

Lucy held his stare for a moment. There was nothing to be gained by being pig-headed. She let out a sigh.

'All right. I suppose that would suit.'

'I'll wait in the car for you.'

Lucy watched as he sauntered out of the room, broad-shouldered and confident.

Pop had been resting comfortably after the operation, and the doctor had said he'd be home by the weekend. Unlike Gran, he didn't hide his tears when her three cousins had walked in. He was still wiping his eyes when Lucy slipped into the room.

The room was full of laughter, and even Gran smiled at some of Pop's endless jokes.

'Did I tell you about—'

'I've got to go, Pops,' Lucy interrupted. 'I've got a few chores to do, and I'm getting a lift home.' She leaned over and hugged him, inhaling his familiar scent.

Liam followed her out into the corridor. 'How are you getting home?'

'With Garth.'

Liam's eyebrows rose in a scowl, and she grabbed his arm and pulled him to the side of the corridor.

'Enough with the beetling brows, Liam. Why do you always think the worst? I'm going to find out what Garth is up to,' she whispered as Gran's head poked out into the corridor. 'Jeez, she never misses a trick, does she!'

'What do you need to talk to him about? I was going to call and let him know the place is not for sale.'

'I want to know for sure before I commit to anything. Maybe it's a solution we should keep in the back of our minds.'

'I thought we'd *all* committed?' Liam took her arm and kept his voice low. 'If you're going to change your mind, you'd better do it mighty quick. Didn't you see how happy Pop looked when Gran told him the plan?'

'Yes, I did. I mean, I'm sure, but I'm still worried. I love living in the city. I'm not a country girl anymore.'

'You know what they say, Luce.' Liam's face finally split into a smile. 'You can take the girl out of the country, but you can't take the country out of the girl.'

'Yeah, and this girl loves the city.' Confusion ran through Lucy, and her voice rose louder. 'I want to see what Garth's up to because you heard Gran. If we said no, she would have sold up to him.' She frowned. 'And where would he get the money for that? Cattle prices haven't been that good, have they?'

'You'd know better than me. I've been overseas, remember?'

'Will you two stop sniping! I can hear you all the way down the hall.' Sebastian stepped from the room and walked across to them. 'Pop thinks you're fighting, and now he's reminiscing about when we were all kids.

'Lucy's staying in town with McKenzie.'

Solidarity hummed between Liam and Sebastian for the first time as Seb scowled at Lucy, too.

'Why?'

'Oh no, don't you start on me too.' She slowed down and let them walk ahead. 'I'll see you both at home later.'

##

Garth was waiting for her in the car park, leaning casually on his red-dust-covered ute, his Akubra pulled low over his eyes to block out the late afternoon sun. Lucy swatted at the sticky flies that buzzed around her and wiped away the trickle of perspiration that ran down her neck as soon as she stepped out of the cool, air-conditioned hospital.

Great. Dust *and* flies. The only thing missing to make it perfect—not—was the prickles, she thought crossly. Garth pushed himself off the bull bar as she walked across, and he opened the passenger door for her. Lucy was in a strange mood; Sebastian and Liam had made her cross with their inquisition, and the surge of pleasure that ran through her as Garth helped her up into the ute cab added to her ill temper. What was a girl to do? Why was she the only one seeming to be in this position? It wasn't fair.

'The milk bar or the RSL club?' Garth looked across at her as he started the ute, and the rattle of the diesel engine filled the cabin.

'I don't care.' She shrugged. 'You know the town better than me these days.'

'Okay, RSL it is. They've got a coffee shop out the back, overlooking the river.' He pulled out of the car park, and Lucy was aware of a few looks directed their way as he drove down the main street. Another mark against small country towns in her books. In the city, you could be anonymous. In the country, everyone knew your business. The way the grapevine worked here, she and Garth would be married with three kids by the time the day was over. Lucy gave a polite smile as Mrs Jones from the CWA stood and stared at the ute as they drove past.

'The river, you said?' She squinted and looked over the side of the bridge that split the town in half. Cracked mud and dead grass stretched as far as she could see.

'Okay, the riverbed. There's been no water in the river for a couple of years now. The drought's got a big hold at this end of the Pilliga. Unfortunately, the bores don't stretch as far as town. There are a lot of property owners doing it very tough here now, Lucy.'

The RSL was a small brick building on the other side of the river—riverbed—and the car park had begun to fill as the working day ended. Garth waved and greeted a few workmen in fluoro vests as they walked across the car park to the double doors at the top of the steps. The club was noisy, and the doorman greeted Garth as he signed Lucy into the club.

'Looks like you've come home to stay, Garth? I thought you'd be sick of the place after six months.' The man boomed out in a loud voice and Lucy looked at Garth curiously, wondering where he'd been. He caught her glance and smiled. 'Nice to be missed.'

'Where have you been?'

'Oh, here and there,' he said with a cheeky grin. 'Come on, Lucy. Lighten up. You look like the weight of the world is on your shoulders. Tell me more about this sexy underwear gig you want to sign me up for.' He pulled out a chair for her at a table in the coffee shop, and she jumped as his fingers brushed against hers. 'Coffee or tea?'

'Short black, please.' Lucy leaned back in her chair as Garth went to the counter to order. She let her eyes linger on him as he turned away. A professional glance, she told herself. Broad shoulders, muscular thighs and tight jeans that hugged his trim hips completed the sexy picture. His biceps bulged beneath the tight sleeves of his navy-blue T-shirt, and as she admired his physique, Lucy realised that most of the other women in the bistro were doing the same thing. Garth turned around and looked a bit sheepish as he caught her staring. He carried over the coffee and slid her cup across the table before he sat down across from her.

'Thank you.'

'Okay, so what's the go, Lucy-Lou?' His eyes were intent on hers.

'The go?' she repeated.

'What's happening at Prickle Farm? Why the big family visit? No one comes near the place for years, and then all of a sudden, you're all home. Is everyone okay? Harry seems better. What about your Gran?' Despite the concern in his voice, Lucy sensed there was more than sympathy behind his questions.

A sliver of unease ran down her spine. Why was he so interested? It was more than a friendly enquiry. She leaned back and folded her arms. 'So, what's it to you? Are you interested because you want to buy it?'

'I'm interested because I care about my neighbours. They're good people.' His hazel eyes held hers steadily as his deep voice washed over her. 'I thought we were mates, Lucy. Why? Do you think I have some sort of hidden motive?'

'So why *do* you want it?'

Garth ran his hand through his hair in frustration, and she looked up and caught his eyes. The gold flecks were pronounced today, and long, dark eyelashes fringed his eyes. 'The main reason is that I thought it would help your grandparents out because no one else seemed to be interested until you all came rushing home. Your Pop's been struggling; the manager they have is less than useless and—'

'What manager?' she interrupted, her voice almost a squawk. 'Gran didn't say anything about a manager!'

'You haven't met Brian yet?'

'No, she hasn't mentioned any manager.' Lucy frowned. 'I got the impression that she and Pop have been running the place, and the contractors do the harvesting.'

Garth shook his head. 'Lucy, your grandfather's barely been able to walk. Who do you think has been drenching the cattle, getting them in the yard and taking them to the cattle sales? I've helped out as much as I could for a while, but I have my place to run.'

Guilt flooded through Lucy, and she put her elbows on the table with her chin in her hands. 'Look, Garth, the last few days have been really confusing for me. Lots of family decisions are being made, and I don't know how you're involved or why Gran really has it in for you. Maybe you'd like to tell me why that is?'

'Maybe I'd like you to trust me like you used to,' he said enigmatically. He lifted his coffee cup and held her gaze steadily. His eyes were clear and open, and Lucy tried to ignore the little frissons of warmth running rampant in her lower belly as they stared at each other. Garth was the first to look away. 'Hell, Lucy. I hate this.'

'Hate what?' she asked softly.

'Arguing with you.' He shook his head. 'Look, let's just forget the farm for a while. Put it aside until we both calm down. Tell me more about your job. Tell me more about this great idea of yours and what you want me to do.'

Lucy forced aside the worry that Garth's words had raised in her. Someone—whether it was him or Gran— wasn't being totally truthful, and she wondered which one of them it was and why there was a need to lie.

'Okay. Let's talk about my business.' After all, she had her own job to worry about, and this sudden family stuff was forced onto her. 'So do you reckon you can help me out with my campaign?'

'All I have to do is get my photo taken with semi-naked women?' That little warm butterfly beat its wings again in her lower belly as his lips tilted into a huge smile. His eyes crinkled at the corners, and his perfect teeth flashed white as he stared at her. 'Sounds like hard work.'

'Yep, that's all you have to do. And you'll get paid.' Her voice trailed off as his smile disappeared.

'I don't expect to be paid, Lucy. I'm happy to help you out. It'll be fun. So what's the go? The time frame?' He leaned forward, and she caught a whiff of aftershave mingled with perspiration and the earthy smell of man. 'How long are you home for?'

'Home?' She shook her head slowly. 'This isn't home. Sydney's home, although I'll—'

Garth reached out and took her fingers in his. 'Although?'

Lucy lifted her chin and looked at him. Despite having doubts earlier, she knew she could trust him. Garth would never do anything to hurt Gran and Pop, but before she told him anything, she had some questions she'd like answered.

'Let's go back to what we were talking about before. Because before I tell you about my campaign, I have some news. It's all connected.'

'Okay. What's on your mind?'

'Why is Gran cross with you? And why do you want to buy our farm?'

'Our farm?' His eyes were serious now. 'I thought your home was Sydney?'

'It is, but it won't be for a while.' She shook her head, frustrated by his lack of answers. Lucy kept her words measured as she spoke slowly. 'So, does Gran have it in for you?'

Garth spread his hands on the table and looked down at them. 'Because I tried to tell her something she didn't want to hear.'

'And?'

'She didn't believe me, and she accused me of some pretty harsh things. She thinks I have an ulterior motive for making up lies.'

'Garth.' Exasperation filled her voice. 'Will you please tell me what is going on?'

He lifted his head, and his expression was troubled. 'I told your grandmother that I suspect her manager is stealing their cattle, and she didn't believe me.'

CHAPTER 11

Lucy asked Garth to drop her at the front gate, and he leaned over and took her hand before she opened the door. When he'd dropped his bombshell about the cattle theft, she'd quickly finished her coffee and asked him to drive her home. She'd been quiet on the half-hour trip home and still hadn't decided whether to tell him she'd be staying at Prickle Creek Farm for a while. She had some thinking to do, as well as some investigation into his allegation.

'I'll talk to Sebastian about taking some preliminary photos tomorrow afternoon,' she said. 'Just before sunset when the light's a bit softer.'

'Okay.' He squeezed her fingers. 'At my place?'

'How about we meet you down by the bore? I'll get the key and unlock the back gate, and you can come the short way.' She stood and watched until Garth's ute disappeared down the road, and the red dust settled before she walked through the gate, brushing the flies from her face.

The smell of barbequing meat greeted her as she pushed open the gate in the fence. Gran insisted on keeping the working dogs away from the house lawn and her garden. Lucy took a deep breath as she crossed the lawn. The fragrance of the flowers of early spring overlaid the smell of meat. If she ignored the red dust backdrop and looked straight ahead, it was like being in an English cottage garden. Gran had grown up in England and followed Pop to Australia when she was only nineteen. When she was little, Lucy loved to sit on Gran's knee and listen to the story of how they met. They'd both worked as volunteers in a collective community on a kibbutz in Israel. Harry, the young Australian farm boy from Western New South Wales, and Helena, the pretty social butterfly from Notting Hill in London, had fallen in love at first sight.

'He was a fine strapping young man.' Gran had looked affectionately at Pop while a young Lucy was on her knee, enthralled by the story.

'And I still am,' Pop had said with his cheeky smile. But Lucy always remembered the way Gran looked at her Harry back in those days. The love had shown on her face and at that time, Lucy had vowed that she would never get married until she could look at a man like that.

'I missed him so much when he came home to Australia that I followed him to see this Pilliga

Scrub he went on about.' Lucy sighed when Pop bent down to kiss Gran. 'And I fell in love with that too.'

So romantic. They'd had a huge social wedding in London, and Gran had moved to the old farmhouse at Prickle Creek Farm. Lucy had grown up believing in romance and happily ever after, but her recent relationships had soured that belief each time a man had let her down. The men she met in the city were focused on their careers, and she had yet to find one who rated her needs as important as his career.

Memories of how soft and loving Gran had been before she and Pop had lost their three daughters came back to Lucy as she crossed the garden. The lawn was green and lush and edged with nodding May bushes and snapdragons, providing a colourful edge between the graceful white flowers and the emerald green lawn. The scent of lavender filled the air and Lucy picked a head from the bush and rolled it between her fingers as she crossed to the steps. Gran had kept in touch with her English heritage with her beautiful cottage garden.

A rush of love for the sad woman ran through Lucy, and regret that she had stayed away for so long pierced her chest. Voices and laughter met her as she pushed open the back door and stepped into the cool, air-conditioned kitchen. Jemmy was sitting at the bench with Gran, shelling peas, and another wave of nostalgia hit Lucy. Seb and Liam were out on the back verandah, standing companionably by the barbeque. She crossed the room, put her arms around Gran from behind, and kissed her soft cheek. 'I'm sorry, Gran.'

Gran put down the vegetables she was holding and turned to her with a frown.

'Sorry? What for? What have you done?'

'I'm sorry for staying away for so long.' She hugged her grandmother tightly. 'I do love you, you know.'

'And I love you, too. Lucy. All of you.' Gran sniffed and brushed a hand across her eyes. 'I'm sorry for being such a cranky old thing, but I've been worried about Harry . . . the farm.'

Lucy hugged her one more time before she crossed to the sink and washed her hands. 'So green pea and mint salad? Yum!'

Gran put her head down and kept shelling the peas, and Jemmy caught Lucy's eye with a smile and a nod. Dinner was a happier affair, and while they were having a cup of tea—none of that

American coffee rubbish in Gran's house—Lucy broached the subject that had been on her mind.

'Gran, is there a manager on the farm?'

As she watched, Gran's shoulders slumped. 'There is. And that's one of the first things I want you boys to check on. 'I think I might have been a bit harsh on young McKenzie.'

Lucy narrowed her eyes. 'Harsh?'

'I didn't believe him. He came over here a couple of weeks ago, and in a roundabout and polite way, he told me that he suspected Brian was stealing cattle. In the next breath, he offered to buy the farm, and I thought he was trying to undermine Brian for his own purposes.'

Liam leaned forward with a frown. 'And now you think he's telling the truth?'

'As much as I hate to admit it, I think young McKenzie may be right. While you were all down at the bore last night, I had a good look at the books. Harry usually looks after all that, but he's been preoccupied lately, trying to cope with the pain.' Her face wrinkled in a frown, deepening the lines in a complexion ravaged by fifty years of hot western sun. 'There is a huge discrepancy between the calves born last season and the steers sold at the last few sales.'

LUCY

'Maybe he's been fattening them for the next sale? Waiting for prices to go up?'

Three mouths dropped open, and Gran smiled as everyone turned to Sebastian.

'Thus speaks the country boy.' Liam's voice held no sarcasm this time; it was full of admiration.

A flush settled on Seb's high cheekbones. 'Just because I live in the city doesn't mean I've lost touch with the ways of the country.'

'Me neither,' Liam added. 'I checked the cattle prices every day I was in England. Streamed ABC radio on the internet.'

'What about the time difference? Wasn't that the middle of the night over there?' Seb sounded sceptical.

'Midnight in London,' Liam said with a smile. 'Brought me home each night before I went to sleep.'

Seb looked at him thoughtfully, and a smile tilted Gran's lips. 'So you're both well placed to start learning the daily routine. Your grandfather will be very pleased.' She stood, and Seb and Liam jumped to their feet. 'No time like the present. We'll go and look in the office now, and you can tell me whether you think Brian McDermott has been dudding us.'

CHAPTER 12

By nine o'clock the next morning, the manager had been dismissed, and the police had been informed of the missing cattle. Jemima and Lucy were left in charge of the kitchen while Gran set off on horseback to the back paddocks with Liam and Seb cantering beside her. Together, they would see how much stock was left.

'Look at her, Luce. She's better on horseback than the guys are.' Jemima wrapped the scones in the tea towel and placed them in the box. 'Are you still scared of horses?'

'Not scared so much, but I hate being up high on them and not having any control of where they go.' She gave a rueful grin. 'But I guess I'm going to have to get over that as quickly as I can.'

'You know'—Jemima leaned back on the kitchen bench and crossed her arms—'I'm really looking forward to coming back here and spending time back on the farm. I've even been thinking I might move back for good one day.'

'But what about your career?' Surprise filled Lucy as she looked at her cousin's manicured fingers and perfectly styled hair.

LUCY

Jemima shrugged. 'I've done well enough already to set me up for life. You know, I've felt more settled since I've been back here in the last two days than I have for years. I'm over international airports, living out of hotel rooms and parading clothes for the rich and famous.'

'Half your luck. You're younger than me, and my career has only just started to take off. This current deal will set me on the path to success . . . hopefully.' Lucy paused as she filled the last thermos with boiling water. 'But you're right, I think we all needed to come back to get on with the healing. The longer we stayed away, the harder it became.'

'What about you, Lucy? Could you ever come back here to live?'

As Lucy shook her head emphatically, an image of Garth McKenzie's face filled her thoughts. 'No. You know me. The flies, the dust, the prickles.' She waved a hand towards the paddocks they could see through the window. 'Not what I want at all.'

'What about our heritage, the family and'—Jemima bumped her shoulder—'the gorgeous Garth?'

Heat rose into Lucy's face, and she walked away and opened the fridge.

'Garth?' She stalled for time as a little skitter ran down her spine. What was wrong with her? 'We're just friends. And he's going to do a photo shoot for me for my campaign. Oh damn, in all the talking, I forgot to tee it up with Sebastian. Remind me when they come back in for lunch.'

'We'll see,' Jemima said with a grin. 'You didn't see the way your 'just friend' looked at you yesterday.' She put her finger to her chin. 'And I seem to remember hearing about an encounter or two by the dam—'

'That was when we were kids!'

'Kids? You were eighteen, and I remember you were in *lurve*.'

Lucy elbowed Jemmy and grinned as she put the butter in the esky. She was saved from further teasing when the screen door opened.

Tommy Robinson pushed open the door and fell back against the door in a dramatic pose with his hand on his chest. 'Be still my beating heart. Now there's two of them!'

'Come in, Tommy,' Lucy said. 'This is my cousin, Jemima.'

She smiled. It was Jemima's turn to blush as Tommy took her hand and bowed before kissing her fingers.

LUCY

'Love coming over to the kitchen these days,' he said with a cheeky grin.

'I thought the harvesting was almost over,' Lucy said with a frown. Not that she minded; if she was in the kitchen, she didn't have to work outside.

'Another three days will see us out.' Tommy picked up the boxes and, with a final appreciative grin, shot Jemima's way; he headed back to his ute.

Jemima glanced at Lucy as he drove away. 'I can stay that long, and then I'll head back to Sydney and organise my life. How would you like to move into my unit in Mosman when I'm out here? I don't fancy leaving it empty.'

'Really? That would be great. I live in a one-bedroom dump in Newtown that's seen better days, but because it's close to the city, even the rent for that is almost unaffordable.'

'I feel so bad that we live so close and didn't see each other. What happened to us all, Luce?' Jemima looked out at the paddocks with a sigh.

'Tragedy that not many families go through on that scale, I guess. We knew if we got together, we'd have to remember it.'

'You know what? I'm going to saddle up and follow them down the back. Want to come for a ride?' Jemima pulled her loose hair back into a ponytail

Lucy shook her head. 'No thanks! I'll tidy up here and do some more work on my proposal. Can you tell Seb I've lined him up for this afternoon in case I'm not here when they come in?'

'Will do.'

Lucy stood and watched as Jemima headed for the horse paddock, her back straight and her walk graceful. She'd felt like a misfit when they talked about cattle and feed and weights, but never more so than now as she watched Jemima stride confidently to the horses.

##

Lucy spent the afternoon on her laptop, trying to Zoom with the office. The connection kept dropping out, and in the end, she called Caleb onto the landline, and he gave her verbal approval to start the campaign she proposed.

'Flick me an email with the outline, and send me some of the photos you get this afternoon, and I'll have a look. But Lucy, the concept sounds great. Go for it!'

At four-thirty, she looked anxiously at the clock; there was no sign of Gran and her three cousins. Luckily, the food for pickup had been prepared, and all she had to do was pack it and wait for Tommy to collect it when he brought the lunch baskets back in. She smiled as he looked around for Jemima.

'Sorry, Tommy. Only me this time.'

Lucy took a quick shower and deliberated over what she would wear before pulling herself up with a good talking-to. In the city, she'd wear cargos and a T-shirt, so that would do here. The lipstick she put on was purely to stop her lips from getting burned by the late afternoon sun.

It was.

She grabbed a bottle of water and her hat and then scribbled a note for Seb, reminding him to come down to the dam and bring his camera as soon as he could. The cattle crush was quiet and empty when she walked past, but a sudden memory of her mum sitting on the top rail as the cattle ran through the gate made her catch her breath. Lucy took out the memory and let it roll around in her thoughts; back in those days, she loved to help when Mum and Dad came out from town when the cattle work was full-on.

'Move 'em, move 'em along, Paul.' The beasts were noisy, and it was hot and dusty work. Mum was perched up on the rail, her blue-checked flannel shirt flapping in the cool winter wind as Dad pushed the cattle along in the crush. It was Lucy's job to lift the gate and let them out one by one after Mum lifted the drench gun and moved to the next beast. In primary school, she'd felt important, and by the time she'd got to high school, she was allowed to write down the weights as Pop weighed the cattle so the cattle got the right dose of Cydectin. God, she even remembered the name of the drench for parasites in the cattle. What else was buried in her brain?

She shook her head and stared at the cattle crush. The only noise today was the chain rattling on the gate as the hot westerly blew in. If she was honest, it was only after Mum died that she associated Prickle Creek Farm with all the bad memories. Before then, the dust, the flies, the heat and the prickles had just been a part of life and hadn't bothered her.

Her thoughts were pensive as she walked to the back dam.

CHAPTER 13

Garth watched as Lucy strolled along the edge of the dam wall towards him, her head down. He'd come down early and put out some yabbie nets, remembering how much Lucy used to love to fish for the muddy crustaceans. Years ago, he'd stood behind her, holding the string, showing her how to feel the tug and pull the suckers in from the muddy water. She'd been so excited when they pulled the nets in; Garth had been more excited by the press of her soft curves against his chest.

Back in those happy days, it didn't take much to make her smile; these days, she seemed so sad. The only time her face lit up was when she was talking about her work. Her job was in Sydney, six hundred kilometres and a seven-hour drive away. He frowned—even though he'd only spent a small amount of time with her, the thought of Lucy leaving Prickle Creek Farm again was not one he was very keen on.

Maybe he'd spend a bit of time in the big smoke when he got the farm sorted. Keep in touch, go down and visit.

Yeah, and pigs might fly.

There was no future there. He wanted to stay on the farm and get married. Raise a family. There was nothing to be gained by going to the city. He and Lucy wanted different things in life now. He had to remember that and not live on the old memories.

No matter how much he loved that sexy sway of her hips.

Even though the work was hard, Garth knew he'd made the right choice. Six days between Christmas and New Year each year was the only time his parents had ever left the farm for the annual family holiday up to Mooloolaba on the Sunshine Coast. When he'd taken over six months ago, in the excitement of being a landholder, he'd forgotten the long, hard slog and the daily grind of running a five-thousand-acre property. But up until this week, spending all his time on the farm and not being able to get away much hadn't bothered him too much. He loved his farm, and he loved living in the Pilliga Scrub. Hell, he wasn't even going to take the traditional break when the next summer holidays came around, even though Dad had offered to come home and give him a spell. He didn't need one, and he didn't want one. Maybe in a couple more years when he was settled.

'Hey, Garth.' Lucy called down from the top of the levee bank at the edge of the dam.

'Hey, Lucy-Lou.' Garth put down the string he was holding and placed a small rock on it to keep it secure.

'I didn't think you were here yet,' she said with a hand up to her eyes. The sun was setting, and the golden shafts of light reflecting off the dam were bright.

'Came down and parked in the shade a while back.' He nodded to the small stand of trees where he'd parked the ute. 'And then I came down to the water to set some nets.' His eyes ran over her lush curves, moulded by a snug pink T-shirt. 'I remembered how much you enjoyed yabbie fishing.'

'Eww, I forgot about the yabbies in the dam when I swam the other day. No more swimming in that one!'

Garth laughed at the look of horror on her face. 'Come on, they don't bite. Where's my country girl gone?'

Lucy held his gaze, and a strange shimmer ran through him. It was more than desire; it was a strong need to get to know her again, to make her smile and take away those shadows from beneath her eyes. He shook himself mentally and looked past her. 'Where's your photographer?'

Lucy put her hands on her hips and rolled her eyes. 'My fault. They all went out on horseback to check the cattle at the back of the property, and I forgot to ask him. They didn't even come in for lunch. But I left him a note to come out here when they get back.'

Garth kept his eyes on her face, ignoring the clinging T-shirt. 'So while we wait for him, we have time to catch some yabbies.'

He reached up and held out his hand to Lucy at the top of the bank. She grabbed his outstretched fingers, and as she stepped down, her boots sank into the soft side of the dam wall, and the red dust caved in to reveal a network of small holes.

'Good sign; the yabbies have been burrowing in the bank, so there must be a few in the water.'

Lucy followed him over to the water's edge, and Garth glanced across at her. 'Want to pull the first one in?'

Her nod was enthusiastic, and he watched as she gently picked up the rock and tugged at the string.

LUCY

'Feels heavy.' A delighted squeal left her lips as she pulled the string, and the first net cleared the water. 'Oh, look. Five beauties.'

'Dinner. I was hoping you'd come over tonight after you got your photos.' Garth gestured to the ute before he bent and lifted the huge crustaceans out by the back of their shells. He was wary of those huge nippers; he'd had them latch onto him more than once, and it wasn't pretty. 'I threw in a pot, a rack and some rock salt on the off chance we caught some.'

Lucy's smile sent another ripple of need running through him. 'What about your special sauce?'

'You remember?' He looked at her quizzically as he dropped the yabbies into the bucket and snapped the lid on.

'How could I forget such a gourmet delight?' She tilted her head to the side, and he watched as she ran the tip of her tongue over her full pink lips. 'Equal parts of tomato sauce and condensed milk mayonnaise if I remember correctly. Right?'

He held his fingers to his lips in an Italian gesture. 'Spot on, food of the gods.'

'You know, Garth. I used to think about you and that sauce whenever I went to the flash seafood restaurants in the city. Always made me smile.'

'Nice to know you were thinking of me, Luce.' He wiped his wet hands on his jeans, reached up, and cupped her face in his palm. 'I thought of you, too. Often.' He held her gaze steadily, and the soft evening light deepened the mauve shadows beneath her eyes. An unfamiliar surge of protectiveness ran through him. 'Wondered where you'd got to and what you were up to. And I'm proud of you now you're a mover and shaker in the world of advertising. I thought you might go into the music business. I remembered how much you used to love country and western music. Or has that changed now you're a city dweller?'

She grinned at him, 'No way would I give up my music. I haven't missed the Country and Western Festival at Tamworth for the past three years.'

'Oh, you lucky gal. That's still on my bucket list.'

Lucy leaned over and bumped his shoulder with hers. 'And guess who signed my T-shirt last year?'

'Who?' Garth smiled back; her eyes were dancing with excitement.

LUCY

Lucy's voice was sweet as she sang, '*But what's a country girl do for fun, when her working day is done?*'

'No shit?'

Lucy nodded.

'For real? You met Lee Kernaghan?' Garth was impressed. 'You're a city girl, and you still sing C&W?'

'I did, I am, and I have the T-shirt to prove it,' she said with a grin and turned as the sound of an engine came over the levee bank.

'So how about tonight? Wanna come over later?' He tried to keep the neediness out of his voice. *Sheesh, what is wrong with me?* 'It would be nice to have some company.'

'I'll let you know later, okay?'

Garth ignored the disappointment shooting through him. He was overreacting; he was only trying to be helpful.

'Did you ever start the great Australian novel you always said you'd write one day? You were always such a fabulous storyteller at high school.' He watched as she pulled the string again. Another successful haul, and she smiled.

'So the book?' he pressed.

Lucy shook her head but didn't answer his question. She pointed up the hill. 'Oh good, here's Seb now. And the light is just about perfect.'

Garth walked thoughtfully behind her as she clambered up the bank in front of him. He'd been leading too much of a lonely life over the past six months. Combine that with the memory of Lucy lying next to him as they'd spent the afternoons discovering each other on a picnic rug at this very dam; it was no wonder she interested him so much now. That's all it was; he'd get over it when she went back to the city.

He'd have to.

##

Lucy had put aside the novel she'd written in the months following Mum's death. She didn't want to think about it, and she certainly didn't want to talk about it. Reading her words had frightened her; her vulnerabilities and her deepest desires had been exposed in the story that had poured from her and filled the void that grieving had left. She'd put too much of herself into her story. Never for public consumption, not if she wanted to be seen as a confident twenty-four-year-old.

But Garth's words had left lingering warmth in her chest. Not only had he thought about her, but he sounded genuinely pleased that she was making a success of her career, and he'd remembered her writing dream. With any luck, his willingness to be a part of this campaign would contribute to her career success, and she would be well on the way to shaking up the advertising business.

Funny how things came around. Life was strange.

Back here in the Pilliga, and the opportunity she'd sought for so long in Sydney was here right in front of her.

And he was still gorgeous. Too gorgeous for my peace of mind.

The sun was hovering above the horizon and the bank of cloud in the western sky was a deep pink. Seb jumped out of Pop's ute and slung a camera around his neck before sauntering over.

'Not such a bad idea, Lucy. Best light ever, out here.' He held out his hand to Garth and shook it firmly as he greeted him. 'Didn't get much of a chance to say hello the other day, Garth. How's things over at the McKenzie farm?'

Lucy lifted her head and watched, surprised, as Sebastian and Garth chatted about cattle prices. Her eyes narrowed as Seb's voice rose enthusiastically as Garth told him about the rise in prices on the radio at midday.

'Missed that,' he said with a sidelong glance at Lucy. 'We were out on the horses. Ended up mustering the back paddock.'

She stared at him and shook her head with a grin. 'Who is this man?' Her grin turned into a chuckle. 'Aliens have taken my cousin, the photographer. Can you take photos, too?'

Sebastian pulled a face at her. He wore a pair of old work trousers and a khaki shirt. The only hint of the metrosexual from the city was the man bun that Lucy knew was tucked beneath the battered Akubra. He'd even taken the diamond stud out of his ear before he arrived at the farm.

'He's here and he's ready to get to work.' Seb held his camera up. 'Let's go if you want to catch this light.'

Lucy enjoyed the next hour. Positioning Garth against a tree trunk, with the light filtering through the dry leaves behind him, meant she had to run her hands down his muscled arms. Removing his hat, running her fingers along his jaw, tilting his head and mussing his hair sent a tremble to her legs. She swallowed and focused on being professional.

LUCY

Seb clicked away as Lucy instructed Garth where to put his hands.

'And stop smiling.' She stepped back, put her hands on her hips and regarded those sexy lips set in a smile. 'I want you to look rugged yet mysterious. It will be a real contrast to the sexiness of the underwear.'

'Sorry, I can't help it. Never thought I'd find myself in this position.' The quiet confidence in his voice as Garth tried to compose his face into a serious expression put paid to any embarrassment she thought he might have had. He was more professional than most of the models they worked with in the city, and as Lucy lifted a hand to Garth's hair again, Seb winked at her.

'If cattle and wheat prices go down, he can come to work as a model in the city; what do you reckon, Luce?'

She caught Garth's eyes on her, smiled up at him, and nodded. 'Sure could.' Reaching over to adjust the sleeves of his T-shirt, she pushed them up a little so that the curve of his bicep caught the light. Her fingers lingered over his warm skin, smooth and tanned beneath her touch.

As she reached across, he leaned down, and his breath whispered against her ear. 'I hope you're enjoying this as much as I am.'

Heat rushed up her neck at the same time as goosebumps rose where his breath had lifted her hair away from her neck.

She was, and it had nothing to do with the advertising campaign she should be focusing on. Her voice was prim as she hid her response. 'Enjoying what?' she said with a little shrug. 'This is what I do every day.'

Seb chuckled but the look he shot her was intense. 'You wish, Luce.'

Garth leaned against the tree with a smile, just looking bloody beautiful.

'Light's gone.' Seb put his camera down. 'Great work, guys. How are you going to get the shots to the agency, Luce?' They'd despaired of the dodgy internet connection when Seb had tried to download some files that morning.

Garth pushed himself away from the tree trunk and came across to them. 'Feel free to come to my place. Remember I said you can use my connection, and the offer to cook the yabbies is still open, too.'

Lucy nodded. 'Thank you and yes to both, much appreciated.' She was surprised to hear her voice so calm. The feel of Garth's skin and muscles was burning her fingertips and her legs were like jelly. The warm and earthy smell of him wafted over as he moved closer, and she looked up. His T-shirt was now damp with perspiration despite the deepening dusk, and she stared at him, unable to help herself. The shadow of stubble along his jawline and the lock of hair that fell across his brow conspired to keep her eyes fixed on him. He was too good-looking for her peace of mind.

As she watched, he glanced across at Seb, and she wondered if she was the only one to hear the reluctance in Garth's invitation.

'We've got some yabbies here to cook up. Would you like to stay and have some with us?'

To Lucy's relief, Seb shook his head and turned towards the ute. 'Thanks, but no. Gran wants Liam and me to look at the cattle records with her again tonight while the numbers are fresh in our minds.' He glanced back at Lucy and grimaced. 'She's coming around slowly, but I'll warn you, she wasn't too impressed to hear why I had to come out here and meet you.'

Garth gave a rueful grin. 'And I'll have dropped even lower in her opinion.'

'No, Garth. She's going to apologise to you. It didn't take long for her to see that you were right about Brian.' He opened the ute door and placed his camera carefully on the passenger seat. 'So you don't want a lift back, Luce?'

'No, but I won't be long.'

She stood close to Garth as Seb drove off. Once the noise of the motor receded, all was quiet, and she kicked nervously at the dust with her boot. There was a tension between them that had begun as she was touching his skin, and she knew it wouldn't take much for it to burst into flame—on her side, anyway.

'Speaking of flame,' she said and then stopped as a wave of heat flooded her face when she realised she'd put her thoughts into words. 'I mean, do you want me to gather some sticks to start the fire?'

##

When Garth spread the old yellow and black checked picnic blanket on the red dirt, Lucy looked at him from beneath lowered lashes. She could have sworn it was the same one he'd had in his old ute when they'd swum at the dam the summer before he'd left Prickle Creek. After his Year Twelve exams were over, in that glorious summer holiday before Garth had left town, she'd taken every opportunity to spend nights out at Prickle Creek Farm with Gran and Pop. Mum and Dad had teased her; they'd known full well that the attraction was not the farm or her grandparents. It had been an idyllic summer; she and Garth had swum, hiked and fished for yabbies. They'd lain on an old checkered rug, looking at the brilliant stars in the clear night sky and sharing their dreams. They'd tentatively explored each other's bodies and slept under the moon and stars.

The water in the large battered pot was just short of coming to a boil on the crackling flames. Lucy sat and stared into the yellow, gold and blue fire, lost in her memories, while Garth opened the lid on the bucket, and when the bubbles began to rise, he carefully dropped the yabbies into the water. She grinned and glanced down at her watch. It had always been her job to time the cooking.

'Three minutes, I know.' She nodded as Garth held up three fingers. She stood in front of the fire, watching the pot swing on the tripod.

How had I let go of those memories? Of the wonderful times they'd spent together? It was as though the tragedy in their family and the loss of her mother and two aunts had pulled a curtain over that part of her life. She hadn't forgotten those happy weeks; it was just that when Mum had died, she'd pushed anything to do with Prickle Creek and Prickle Creek Farm into a part of her memories that she never ventured into.

Now, sitting out here in the warm night, staring into the flames, the years disappeared, and the curtain shifted a little. She explored the memories; it was like probing a sore tooth. Test and pull back until you knew it wasn't going to hurt anymore. Garth must have sensed her introspection; he pottered around quietly, and she looked at him gratefully when he lifted two camp chairs and a small fold-up table from the back of the ute.

'I remembered how much you hated the cats eyes prickles,' he said with a smile.

Nostalgia flooded through Lucy. How could she have walked away and never called him? Not once had she contacted Garth after she'd moved to Sydney and started her new life. He'd been relegated to the place where she'd grown up, the place she kidded herself she'd hated.

'One minute to go.' She looked at her watch as she sat down in the comfortable chair. Garth lifted an esky from the ute, and she smiled again as he took out a bottle of tomato sauce and a jar of homemade mayonnaise and put them on the table. He reached in again and pulled out a bottle of wine and two glasses.

'You did have this all planned, didn't you? Just as well we caught some yabbies.' Lucy took the glass of wine Garth poured and then held it out to her. She sat back and sipped as he lifted the pot from the fire with a pair of strong pliers and tipped the water down the hill. He placed the now-red yabbies on an enamel plate on the table to cool in the night air before pulling the other chair over beside hers.

The fire crackled and hissed, and Lucy stared into the flames, searching for the right words. Finally, she turned to him. Garth leaned back with his head resting on the high, soft back of the chair, his eyes closed. His profile was sharply defined against the night sky, and a rush of feeling filled Lucy.

'I'm sorry I lost touch with you,' she said softly. 'Everything changed after the accident. I'd only been at uni a few weeks when Mum and her sisters left for that trip.' He turned and looked at her without speaking. 'I guess after it happened, I just wanted to cut all ties with the place.'

'No need to explain, Luce. I was just as slack. I should have come down and seen you or, at the very least, called you.' He turned back to the fire and leaned forward. 'I went to uni in Western Australia that same month. I qualified as an engineer and I worked in the mines over there. I've only been back on the property six months.'

Lucy's eyes widened and she shook her head. 'I had no idea you went to uni.'

As she watched, Garth's expression closed. 'You thought I was just a cow cocky?'

'No. I didn't let myself think about you at all, Garth.'

'I'm sorry. Dad was really unhappy when I said I was leaving the farm to go to uni. I guess I'm still a bit sensitive.'

'That's okay. We all carry stuff from our families.' Lucy looked down as he reached for her hand. 'But now that we've reconnected, I hope we don't lose touch again.'

'We'll make sure we don't.' Garth held onto her hand as they sat quietly, staring into the flames.

Finally, he broke the silence. 'So, tell me, what's going on with your grandparents? How come you're all home? Is everything okay?'

'I don't know.' Lucy shook her head. 'I mean, yes, apart from getting old, everything is fine with them. I just don't know if I'm okay with the way things are going.'

Garth's glance was curious, and she squeezed his hand before she let go and reached for her wine.

'We're all staying here—home—for a few months. To learn about the property and to take it over eventually.'

She saw the glint of his teeth in the firelight as he grinned. 'That's fantastic. You'll be around for—how long?'

'Three months. We're taking it in turns. Liam and I are first.' She spoke slowly as doubt assailed her.

'So, what's wrong?' Garth picked up on her hesitation. 'You don't sound very keen.'

'I think I only agreed to it because the others were so determined to listen to Gran. I mean, I don't want Gran and Pop to sell the place, but I'm not sure it's what I want.' She waved a hand around at the land surrounding them. 'You remember. I hated all this stuff. The heat, the smells, the dust—'

'That's not the Lucy I remember.' His voice was soft and caressing, and she hardened her tone.

'It's the new Lucy after I left and went to Sydney—after I left the district. Really, there was nothing I liked about being out here on the farm when we came out from town.'

'Nothing?' There was a cheeky tone in Garth's voice.

'Well, maybe some of it was okay.' She looked across at him and then put her hand to her mouth. 'Oh no. I totally forgot that you said you had made an offer for the place. You probably don't want us out here anyway.'

Garth pushed himself up from the chair and crouched in front of her, taking her hands in his. The moon was high in the velvet sky and the pale light glinted off his dark hair. She stared at him and his voice was full of passion as he held her gaze.

'No, don't ever think that. Yes, I could expand my land holdings, but I just didn't want to see the farm go to one of those big foreign investors. That's why I made the offer.'

'What do you mean?'

'Half of the Pilliga is being bought up quietly. There's coal seam gas exploration happening and these companies can see a huge profit in owning land out here.'

'But they can't do that.' Lucy was filled with dismay. 'You mean put mines like there are all over the Hunter Valley out here in the Pilliga?'

'Not quite open-cut mines here, but it will still have a dreadful effect on the water table. But there is talk of open-cut mines out on the Breeza Plains. I've joined a farmers' alliance group and some of the proposals would make your hair curl.' He shook his head. 'And it's all kept very quiet until it's too late to do anything. I'll get Liam and Seb on board too. I'm sure they haven't heard about it. It's all very hush-hush.'

'That's dreadful.' Lucy squeezed his hands. 'But how could you afford to buy a property the size of ours?'

'I've got the approval from the bank, but if the place is staying in your family, that's fine. I really have enough on my plate with mine, and I don't want to have to hire anyone to help out after harvest. I've got a couple of young guys who come out after school and on weekends, and that's all I need with my place.'

'You do love it here, don't you?'

'It's my life,' he said. 'I missed it so much when I was over in the west.' He grinned at her as he stood and pulled her to her feet. 'There's no place like home, Dorothy. Come on, your yabbie feast awaits.'

He brushed a light kiss on her lips and dropped his hands to her hips. He held her gently, and Lucy stared up at him as he lifted his head. Garth smiled at her, and desire quivered in her tummy. He dropped his head again, and this time, her lips clung to his until he moved back and turned his attention to the now cool yabbies. Lucy put her hands to her lips. She couldn't imagine Garth anywhere but here.

The question was, where was home for her?

CHAPTER 14

The outside security light bathed the new farmhouse and the work shed in bright white light as Garth turned the ute into the parking bay close to the house gate.

'You built the new house?' Lucy had asked as they drove past the old farmhouse. They'd called into Prickle Creek Farm on the way home and picked up her laptop and the memory card from Seb's camera. Garth had waited in the ute while Lucy had run inside.

'Yep. Wanted a place of my own. Made it feel as though it was my place and I wasn't just back where I grew up.' He shrugged. 'I know it sounds silly, but I'm going to make my life here, and I wanted it to be mine. You know, not feel like a kid playing on Mum and Dad's farm? And the harvesters bunk down in the old house. And I'm thinking about doing it up a bit and having farm stays there for city kids who wouldn't get a chance for a holiday.'

'Sounds like you've got some great plans for the place.' Lucy looked at him with her head tilted to the side. 'You'll be putting a lot of your time and money into the farm.'

Garth sensed the question in her words; he hated sounding like he was building himself up but he wanted Lucy to know he was comfortable—more than comfortable. 'I did okay over in the west; I worked hard for five years. Instead of flying back home for the two weeks after my shift in the mine, I worked on a wheat farm over there. Set me up to buy the olds' place and left me some spare cash to try some new things.' He didn't mention his shrewd investments. It sounded enough like bragging as it was.

The dogs set up a cacophony of barking in the yard, and he turned to them, relieved to stop talking about himself.

'Quiet,' he yelled, and the three kelpies slunk off to their kennels, surprised by the unfamiliar reprimand.

Garth held out his hand for Lucy to pass her computer down to him before she stepped down from the high vehicle. She was a petite woman, and a surge of longing filled him. Damn shame she was so keen on going back to the city. He blocked the picture in his mind of her living here. That wasn't going to happen.

He held open the gate for her, and she walked into the yard and looked around. A couple of pots filled with dead, straggly plants leaned against the unpainted timber fence.

'Bit different to your Gran's beautiful garden.' Garth shrugged. 'As much as I'd like to get it nice, there's not enough time in a day for me to look after the whole farm, let alone the garden.'

'Are you sure you've got time for me to be here tonight?'

'Of course. I'll get you set up, and I can do some paperwork while you do whatever you have to do. That's one thing I made sure I had: a fast internet connection. My router is hardwired into an antenna on the roof. Picks up the satellite connection twenty-four seven.'

He chuckled at the look on Lucy's face. 'What do we have here? A non-techno person?'

'My nickname at work is 'technogumby', she said with a smile. 'I can use the graphics and word processing software and send an email but that's about it. I can use what I need to do, but I don't understand how it works.' She put one hand on her hip and waved the other in the air. 'It's because I am a *creative* person. I have an aura where computers are concerned. And it's not a productive one.'

She giggled in a self-deprecating way, and Garth smiled along with her. She was so cute and quirky. More and more of the Lucy he remembered from school days was coming back.

'Remember Mrs Johnson, the art teacher?' he said. 'You were the class pet, and she encouraged you when you decided you weren't going to wear the school uniform anymore. I can still remember the look on the headmaster's face when you came to school wearing two different coloured stockings, and your Doc Martens, and that short little pink skirt. I thought he was going to have a stroke on the spot. His face turned the same colour as your boots.

'I'd forgotten that.' Her smile was even wider now. 'And you know what? I've still got those purple Doc Martens.'

They walked through the kitchen to the adjacent open-plan study where Garth had set up his desk. A surge of pride ran through him as Lucy cast an approving eye over the space.

'Very nice. Who designed the house? It's so unusual.'

'I had a mate over in W.A. who worked at the mine with me. He was an architect doing some design work over there. I told him what I was planning and we drew it up between shifts.

It's designed to be naturally temperature-controlled.'

Lucy's eyes tracked along the slope of the ceiling to the storage loft above the laundry. 'I love it. It's almost Japanese, with all the screens.'

'Still a bit bare, but I'll get there.'

'In your spare time,' she said with another laugh.

'That's about right.' He cleared a space on the desk and pointed to the power point above the desk. 'You get yourself set up and I'll put some coffee on.'

He held the chair out for her, and Lucy pulled the small computer from her bag and sat down. 'Coffee will be great. I am a bit sleepy and I have got a lot of work to do. Gran's kept me busy, but you know—I've enjoyed being with her and Jemmy in the kitchen.' Her smile was sweet, and Garth caught his breath as she looked up at him. 'And thanks so much for letting me use your connection. I really do appreciate it.'

'Truth be known, I'll appreciate the company too. Gets a bit quiet here at night.' He laughed as the dogs started barking outside as if on cue. 'Apart from the dogs, that is.'

'Another visitor?' she asked.

'No, it'll be kangaroos. They come in about this time every night and feed on the new growth where I'm trying to get the lawn growing.' He spread his palms open and grimaced. 'Between the dogs and the roos, I think I'm going to be living on red dust for a while.'

'You need Gran over here with her magic touch.' Her expression was shy as she returned his gaze. 'Or if you would like, I can repay you for using your connection and come over and help out with the garden.'

Satisfaction spread through Garth. 'I'll take you up on that.' He held out his hand and took hers. 'That's a deal.'

He had to fight the urge to punch the air with delight as he walked over to the kitchen.

##

'Done.' Lucy stretched her arms into the air and rolled her neck in a circle as the last file whizzed its magical way to Sydney by email. Seb had done an amazing job with the photos of Garth, and she'd worked on the best six and tweaked them before sending them off to the boss with the initial copy she'd written. Fingers crossed that Caleb loved it as much as she did. It might soften him up for when she told him she'd be working from six hundred kilometres away from the office.

'I think we've got a winner of a campaign coming together here.' She turned to the other side of the desk where Garth had been working behind her, but the chair was empty. She'd been so focused on her work that she hadn't even heard him refill her coffee mug; every time she'd picked it up, her cup had been full and piping hot. She pushed the chair back carefully, aware of scratching the polished timber floor, but the chair slid back without any noise. Like everything else she had seen in his house, it had been well thought out and was of the best quality.

Her breath caught as she looked around the room. Garth was on his back on the burgundy Chesterfield beneath the window, one arm flung behind his head. His eyes were closed and his chest rose and fell gently as he breathed. Lucy walked over and stood above him; he was fast asleep. His hair, in need of a trim, curled softly over the neck of his T-shirt. His long, dark lashes rested on his tanned cheeks and his lips were soft and relaxed and her fingers itched to smooth his hair from his forehead.

A flood of longing gripped Lucy and warmth fluttered in her lower belly. A shared look between them was all it had taken to get her feeling like that. With Garth lying there, looking so innocent and attractive, a powerful surge of desire rocked through her. When she'd been a teenager, she'd blamed the constant need to touch him on rampant hormones. This time, she knew it was the attraction he held for her as a man.

He was kind and considerate, thoughtful, and a very giving person. She'd sensed his embarrassment when he'd talked about his work, yet he should be proud of what he'd achieved and of his plans for the future.

Garth McKenzie was a good man. And one who was going to be very hard to leave behind when she went back to Sydney in just over three months' time. Lucy yawned and put her hand over her mouth. It wouldn't be fair to wake him up and expect him to drive her home. She crossed to the kitchen and opened the door quietly before stepping onto the verandah and pulling her phone out.

CHAPTER 15

Garth's internal body clock always woke him before sunrise each morning. He woke with a start this morning as the first rosy tinge of dawn tinted the sky. The ceiling fan was swirling lazily, and he yawned as he watched it. He lay there for a moment and then jumped up when he remembered Lucy.

'Shit,' he muttered beneath his breath. He'd hit the couch for a five-minute nap last night and must have gone out like the dead.

He crossed to the window, but his ute was still there. Lucy hadn't borrowed it, and he hoped she still had enough country savvy not to walk home last night. Her computer was still plugged into the wall and open on his desk, and Garth ran his hand through his hair in frustration.

How did she get home? Bloody hell, how rude can a man be?

He padded silently to the kitchen and looked around. Both of the coffee mugs had been rinsed and were draining on the sink. He frowned. Her bag was still on the bench where she'd left it last night, and a smile crossed his face. Her boots were by the back door where she'd slipped them off last night.

He crept up the hallway and checked the guest room, where there was a queen-sized bed. He'd never made it up, but the bed was empty. He pushed open the door of the second bedroom, where there were two single beds, but they were both empty, too.

With a frown and hope unfurling in his chest, Garth pushed open the door to his room. Cool air from the spinning fan greeted him, and he peered into the dim room; the blinds were closed. He closed the door quietly behind him and walked across to the bed. A bare, slender leg greeted him where the sheet had been pushed back. Lucy lay on her side, her cheek resting in her hand. As he watched, her eyes opened slowly, and she stared up at him.

'Good morning, Goldilocks.' His voice was husky as he met her gaze.

'I hope you don't mind me sleeping over. I didn't have the heart to wake you up last night. It was after midnight when I pulled the pin.'

Garth sat on the edge of the bed and reached over to push her tousled hair back from her rosy cheeks. 'Not at all. I'm sorry I was such a rude

LUCY

host.' He frowned. 'Won't they be worried over at Prickle Creek?'

Lucy rolled over onto her back and stretched. Garth tried hard not to look at the round breasts clearly outlined by her tight T-shirt. He looked away and his attention landed on her jeans lying on the floor beside the bed.

Bloody hell. Lucy Peterkin was in *his* bed and semi-naked.

'No, I called Jemmy and told her I was staying the night.'

'But won't they think—'

Lucy sat up and put her finger over his lips. 'Ssh, I'm a big girl now. If I want to spend the night in a man's bed, that's my choice. Nothing to do with anyone else.' Now, her voice was husky and held a teasing note that sent his blood pressure rocketing up near the fan.

He lifted his hand and held her fingers against his face. Slowly and gently, he turned it over and placed his lips on her open palm. Her skin was warm as he murmured against it. 'No one else? What about the man? Does he get a say in the matter?'

'Depends on whether the man wanted me in his bed or not.'

'Hmm, let me think.' Garth ran his hand along her arm until his fingers reached around to the back of her neck, and he gently tipped her head back until her eyes met his. 'I guess it depends on whether the lady wants to be there or not.' With each word, he moved his head closer and watched as Lucy's lips parted.

'I think she does,' was the reply he wanted to hear. Garth let his lips hover over hers, her breath warming his lips.

'I think she's got too many clothes on,' he whispered.

'I think *he* has too.' Eye to eye, his breathing quickened as Lucy dropped her hands to the bottom of his T-shirt and pulled it up slowly. When his chest was bare, he reached for hers.

'Fair's fair.' Her body was soft, pliant against his, and he drew a shuddering breath as he lifted his head. It had been a few months since he'd last been with a woman, but it was more than the time between sexual encounters that was fuelling this need in him.

'Are you sure, Lucy-Lou?' His voice was throaty with need, and he held her gaze.

'I'm sure.'

With an almighty effort, he stepped back and shook his head. 'We've got plenty of time.'

LUCY

Her mouth was soft beneath his, their first real kiss for so long bringing memories of her sweetness; no one had ever come close to Lucy. He ran his lips over her mouth, her cheeks and her forehead before pressing kisses on her eyelids. Aching with need, he took a deep breath as he lifted his head.

CHAPTER 16

The second time Garth woke up that morning was the most satisfying.

He smiled and glanced at the clock on the wall beyond the end of the bed.

'Damn, look at the time.' He brushed a kiss along Lucy's lips and sat up. 'As much as I want to stay here all day, we're going to have to move. I've got to go over and talk to the contractors. They're due to finish up this afternoon.'

He headed for the shower and smiled as Lucy padded along behind him. He switched on the jets, thanking his designer for advising a shower built for two with the biggest shower head you could buy. When she opened the door and joined him, her expression was cheeky.

No matter what it took, he wasn't going to let her go.

##

Lucy stood in the kitchen as the bright morning sunshine flooded the room. Even though they had made love, slept and then had an extended shower, it was still only eight o'clock. Probably late for Garth to start his day, but if she was at home, she'd only be having her first coffee on the balcony of her tiny little apartment before she headed for work, looking down on the crowds crossing the road and the smell of petrol fumes drifting up to her.

She stared out at the sweeping paddocks as far as she could see. The horizon was distant, and the land was flat and brown, where the wheat had been harvested, broken only by the red ribbons of dusty roads. The difference between her usual start to the day and this one was worlds apart.

And not only because of the time with Garth.

She put what had happened between them this morning in a special place in her thoughts, and when she got back to the farm, she was going to think more about what had happened so naturally between them.

The difference was the environment and the pace of life. There was no noisy traffic roaring past, and the air was fresh and pure. The silence was broken only by the bellow of a beast rubbing up against the fence and the barking of the dogs as Garth went out to feed them.

She turned away from the window, crossed to the kitchen, and switched on the fancy coffee maker as the door opened and Garth came back inside.

'The dogs were most indignant about their late breakfast.' He shot her a lazy grin. 'I told them it was your fault.'

'I need breakfast, too.' She opened the fridge and peered in. 'Got any yoghurt?'

'Nope. But I've got bacon and eggs.'

'No thanks. Not for me.'

Lucy munched on a piece of toast and watched as Garth devoured three poached eggs and four strips of bacon.

'What are you looking at?' He grinned at her as he munched, and she shook her head. The atmosphere between them was light-hearted and comfortable.

'If I ate that much, I'd be the size of a house in a week.'

Garth drained his coffee and stood up. 'It's because I work hard all day while you swan around the city.'

She nudged him, knowing he was only teasing her.

'Come on, lazybones. Sorry to rush you, but I'll run you back home, and then I'll head down the back. The contractors will wonder where I've got to. They'll send a search party out soon.'

Lucy crossed to the desk and unplugged her computer. Her email had downloaded while

Garth was getting dressed; she'd look at them once she got home. Although Gran was certain to have some jobs lined up for her to do first.

Her bag rested against the door while she slipped her boots on. 'I'm ready.'

'One more kiss before we go.' Garth's lips were soft and gentle against hers, and his hands held her lightly. 'Come back over tonight? I'll cook you a real dinner this time.'

Hesitation laced her words; things were moving a bit fast, and she needed to pull back a bit. 'I'm not sure.'

'Why not? I'll cook a lamb roast for you.' His smile tore at her heart, but he was moving way too fast.

'Thanks. But no.' She shook her head.

Disappointment crossed his face, and she relented. If she'd spent the night with him, it didn't mean she was going to have to spend the rest of her life out here in the country.

'All right, you talked me into it, but one thing, Garth.'

'Hit me with it.' His grin was wide.

'No expectations. Okay?'

'Clear as a bell.'

She hoped that he meant that, and didn't have any plans to try and change her mind. If he stuck to his word, the next three months would be more than bearable.

A secret smile tilted her lips. Way more than bearable.

CHAPTER 17

'Have a good night, Luce?' Seb looked like the cat who'd swallowed the cream as the screen door slammed behind her. 'Get all your work done?'

Her three cousins and her grandmother were all sitting at the kitchen table finishing off their cereal and toast. No bacon and eggs in this house. Maybe she'd have to think about cooking a hot brekkie for the boys before they went out to work each day.

Lucy had lived by herself since she'd moved to Sydney, and she wasn't used to 'the morning after' post-mortems, not by anyone, not unless she'd chosen to share her private life with a close girlfriend, which she hadn't done very often.

And certainly not with her cousins, and even worse, not with her grandmother.

God forbid!

'Yes, I got a lot of work done over there.' Lucy ignored his teasing. 'It was late when I finished my work, and Garth had gone to bed, so I bunked down over there.'

Just a little white lie.

Heat ran up her neck as Liam stood and crossed to the sink with his cereal bowl, flicking the side of her face with his finger on his way past.

'Nasty rash you've got on your neck there, Luce. Tell Garth to buy some softer pillowcases.' He turned back to her with a knowing smile.

'Or if needs be, I can lend him a razor.'

'Oooh. You two. Stop teasing.' Lucy glared at them, but her lips twitched. Being an only child, her cousins had teased her constantly as they'd grown up and even though it had been a few years, she was well used to it.

And she loved them for it.

'Half her luck, I say.' Jemmy's voice was soft as she looked up over her tea cup. 'Any more gorgeous neighbours live nearby?'

Lucy closed her eyes as Gran chimed in. 'Leave the girl alone, you lot. It's her business who she wants to sleep with.'

Heat flooded Lucy's face, and she crossed to the sink, hands shaking as she filled a glass with water trying to regain her composure. She felt about sixteen years old again.

Gran continued, and Lucy almost dropped the glass in the sink. 'Although Garth McKenzie has certainly grown into a studly young man.'

LUCY

Seb and Liam howled with laughter. 'Way to go, Gran!'

'Studly!' Jemmy's laugh joined the hilarity. 'Oh, Gran, I love that word.'

'And you tell that young man of yours I owe him a big apology,' Gran said. 'I was too quick to judge him. Invite him over for dinner tonight.'

Lucy put the glass down and turned to find four happy faces, all grinning at her. One week she'd been here, and it was the first time Gran had really smiled. She could put up with their teasing just to see that.

'I will, and then you can tell him yourself.' And then Garth could put up with some of the teasing. 'What's the plan for today?' she asked brightly.

'The boys are going to the back paddock to bring in the cattle we mustered yesterday, and then you girls can help weigh and drench.' This time, Gran's expression was challenging as she looked at Lucy.

'Great, I used to love helping Mum and Dad when they came out to work in the yards with Pop.'

Gran's expression didn't falter at the mention of Lucy's mum; things were looking up. Gran didn't like any mention of the past. If Gran and Jemima could put up with the outside farm work, she'd do her best, too.

'But while they're out mustering the other paddock, we are going to spend the morning baking.' Gran's smile got even wider. 'The hospital just called. Harry's coming home late this afternoon.'

'Oh, that's fabulous news.' Lucy and Jemima smiled at each other.

'So, get your skates on, girls. We're going to cook up a storm.' This time, she looked over the top of her glasses at Lucy. 'And we're getting a later-than-normal start.

'Can we make your famous chocolate cake?' Lucy widened her eyes as she changed the subject from her late arrival home. 'Please, Gran, that cake is to die for.'

Gran nodded and pulled a piece of torn and stained paper from the pocket of her apron. 'I've already got the recipe out for you two. I know it off by heart.'

Lucy scurried off to the bedroom to drop off her laptop and wash her face to try and relieve the flush of embarrassment.

The atmosphere in the kitchen lightened as they greased pans and weighed ingredients. Lucy looked at Jemmy as she washed bowls between cakes. The painted nails were gone, her hair was loose and a smudge of flour dusted her cheek, and she was humming along with the radio as she worked. No one would recognise Jemima Smythe of the Milan catwalk.

Dust was tinting the horizon in the far paddock where Liam and Seb were out on horseback. Their laughter drifted in from the horse paddock as they'd saddled up together. Prickle Creek Farm was healing each of them in different ways; what was it doing for her? She stood there gazing out the window, daydreaming about the night with Garth as the smell of freshly baked chocolate cake filled the kitchen.

'Ice the damn cake!' Gran's voice broke into Lucy's reverie, and her head flew up. Jemima's eyes were wide as she stared at Gran.

'I beg your pardon, Gran?' Lucy said with a frown. No one had ever heard a swear word cross Gran's lips, and Lucy and Jemima looked from Gran to each other until a little giggle came from their grandmother. 'What did you say, Gran?'

Gran held up the recipe and waved the paper at them.

'See, the last line of the recipe says: cream the icing sugar and butter, and then 'ice the damn cake'.'

Lucy crossed over to Gran, wrapped her arms around her, and dropped her head on Gran's shoulder. 'Oh, Gran, it's so wonderful to hear you laugh.' Lucy fought back a sniff as tears threatened.

'And it's good to have you all home.' Gran patted Lucy briskly on the back. 'And I can laugh now that—' Gran's shoulders sagged as she relaxed in Lucy's arms, and her voice broke.

'What's wrong?' Lucy looked up at Jemima as fear chilled her blood. What else did Gran have to tell them? Was there more bad news to be imparted?

'Gran?' Jemima hurried across from the sink, wiping her hands on a towel before throwing it on the countertop.

Gran shook her head and dug into her pocket for a white lace-edged handkerchief.

No tissues for her, Lucy thought, even as worry flooded through her.

Their grandmother pulled away from Lucy's arms, sat at the table, and dropped her head into her hands as sobs wracked her tiny frame. Lucy and Jemima stood beside her, staring at each other in alarm, each with a hand on her shoulders as Gran sobbed into her handkerchief. Great gasping sobs came from her mouth, and she drew in deep breaths between each sob. Lucy crouched down and took the clean towel that Jemima pulled from the drawer and gently wiped Gran's face. Jemima held their grandmother's hand. Lucy clenched her teeth as her throat ached with unshed tears. Finally, Gran spoke, and her voice was hoarse and trembling.

'I was so scared when Harry went to hospital. It brought back all of the memories of your mothers' deaths. I was so sure he was going to die. I honestly didn't know what I would do.'

'But Gran, it was only a simple knee operation.'

Gran lifted her head, and her eyes were fierce. 'Yes, but we're *old*.'

Lucy let the first tear roll down her cheek as Gran reached for her hand and gripped it tightly.

'I couldn't live without Harry. Since he's been in hospital, it's the first time we've ever had a night apart. *Ever*. We've been together since I met him in Israel. I followed back to the Pilliga, and I didn't even go home to London until we went there together for the wedding.' Her hand shook as she lifted the handkerchief and dabbed at her eyes. 'Every decision since then, every moment of happiness has been shared with him, as well as the horror of losing our three daughters. I couldn't bear it if I lost him too. I lay there every night, imagining he wouldn't come back to me. My life would be over, too.'

Lucy tilted her grandmother's chin gently and looked at her. Gran's eyes were red-rimmed, and her chin trembled. 'Today is for a celebration, Gran. Pop's coming home, and we're all here to be with you both.' She took a deep breath. 'I know Mum, and Aunty Carol, and Aunty Jean would be happy if they knew that we were all here and that the farm was staying in our family.

Lucy firmed her voice. '*Our* farm, *our* family. Let's have a fabulous party tonight.'

Gran stared back at her. 'But I still want you to invite your young man.'

'My young man? Gran, Garth and I are friends, nothing more. He's helping me with some work.' Lucy shook her head as heat ran into her face. 'No, tonight is for family. I'll ring Garth and tell him I'll see him later in the week.'

Jemima took Gran's other arm. 'I think you need a lie-down and a lovely bath before Pop gets home. And then I'll get out some of my war paint, find you a pretty dress, and we'll doll you up.'

LUCY

'I don't think so.' Gran laughed, back to her usual pragmatic self. 'A Bex and a lie down will do me, and then we've got to drench those beasts before the boys go to town to get Harry.

Lucy sat down at the table with her head in her hands as Jemmy took Gran down the hall to her bedroom. The power of love was an amazing thing. For the first time in her life, Lucy craved to be loved like that.

But not out here in the red dust.

Garth's face stayed in her head as she crossed to the sink and finished the dishes.

CHAPTER 18

As it turned out, Lucy didn't have to ring Garth after all. She was perched on the rail at the cattle crush, holding a clipboard and writing down the weights. Jemima read the scales and called the cattle weights out to Lucy over the thundering hooves and baying of the beasts, who weren't too impressed with being penned in. Liam was cutting them out, and Seb had the drench gun. Gran was on horseback, guiding them into the adjacent paddock after they were drenched.

'Nice look, Lucy-Lou.' Garth's hand curved around her waist and Lucy grabbed for the rail, almost falling backwards before he held her steady.

'Whoa, just what I wanted. A gorgeous woman falling into my arms.' His voice was deep, and a tremble ran down her back.

'Hi there,' she said shyly. Being up close and personal with him had been in her mind since he'd dropped her off this morning, but having turned up before she was ready threw her for a six. 'I was going to call you when we finished here. I can't come over tonight.'

LUCY

'I know.' He gestured back to Gran. 'You're having a welcome home party for Harry. Your gran's already asked me to come over.'

'Did she?'

'Yeah. Liam and Seb are taking her into Prickle Creek to collect Harry, and she asked me to get the spit going and cook the roasts while they're in town.' He looked at her curiously. 'Is that okay with you?'

'Yes, yes. It's cool. I'd love you to come over. I was just worried that you might feel a bit uncomfortable with Gran being the way she was.'

He shook his head. 'She called me at lunchtime, and we had a long chat. She apologised to me, and I said it was fine. No problem. No hard feelings.'

Lucy pursed her lips. Wily old Gran must have rung from the bedroom when she said she was going to have a lie-down. 'That's good then.'

'Two hundred and seventy-five!' Jemmy's voice registered on Lucy's hearing as she stared down at Garth. 'Lucy! The next one's coming through. Quick!'

'I'll leave you to it.' Garth climbed the bottom rung, reached around, and pulled Lucy's head down to his, and kissed her hard and fast. 'Sorry. I couldn't wait any longer to kiss you.' His grin was cheeky. 'I might walk over for dinner, and maybe you can drive me home later?'

He winked, and those damned butterflies in Lucy's stomach set up a rapid fluttering, but she couldn't help the goofy smile she knew was on her face as she wrote down the next weight. Jemima rolled her eyes but she was smiling too.

##

The welcome home for Harry Bellamy, much-loved husband, grandfather, neighbour and friend, was noisy and boisterous. Garth sat back and smiled as the four cousins argued, Harry told jokes, and Helena sat there with a permanent smile stuck on her face as she stared at her husband. The table was set with a lace cloth, the good china and crystal wine glasses had been pulled out of the Welsh dresser, and the smell of the good country feast enticed them all to eat way too much. Harry sat back and emitted a loud belch, and Helena tapped his arm. But the look in her eyes was loving as she chastised him.

'Harry! I hope you didn't do that in the hospital.'

'Sorry, love. Just showing my appreciation for a grand feast.' He put his fingers over hers and held them. 'And no, the food was crap there. Did I tell you about the time—'

'Harry . . .' Helena said.

Everyone looked at the older couple as they smiled at each other.

But it was Lucy that Garth couldn't keep his eyes off. Her dark hair was pulled up into a twirl thing on top of her head, and she'd done something with her pretty eyes that made them look all dark and mysterious. The three women wore dresses, and Lucy's dangly silver earrings caught the light every time she turned her head to him.

Which, he smiled as he thought to himself, was as often as he looked at her. She was beautiful, and his gut clenched as he stared at her. He grinned as Liam nudged Sebastian and gestured towards Garth with a nod. Sebastian rolled his eyes.

'He's a goner, mate,' he said just loud enough for Garth to hear. 'We'll have to warn him.'

'What are you two up to?' Lucy frowned at her cousins.

'Nothing. Just talking about whose turn it is to do the dishes,' Liam said with an innocent smile in her direction.

Helena pushed herself to her feet and waved at her two grandsons. 'Jemmy and Lucy cooked this feast with Garth's help, so you pair are on kitchen duty. Jemima, you can help me get Harry up the hall, and Lucy can drive Garth home.'

Harry winked at him, and Garth smiled back as Liam and Sebastian cleared the table.

'Thanks for helping us out, Garth.' Lucy's grandfather had been a good support to him when he'd first arrived home, and his parents had headed east. Always willing to share and give good advice, he was sure the misunderstanding about the manager wouldn't have happened if Harry had been home. He'd pulled Garth aside before dinner and thanked him for alerting them about the cattle theft. 'Helena feels bad that she thought you had ulterior motives. She's been in a bit of a state since I went to the hospital and came up with this scheme by herself. It was done and dusted before I even got wind of it.'

'Scheme?'

'For the grandkids to come home and take over.' Harry had nodded to the kitchen where Lucy and Jemima had been helping Gran put the final touches on the meal. Liam and Seb were checking on the cattle and locking the dogs away.

'Ah, yes. Lucy told me.' He was hard-pressed to keep the grin off his face. 'You must be pleased to have the family home.'

'I am.' Worry niggled at him when Harry lowered his voice. 'I'm not convinced it's such a good idea for all of them, though. I think Lucy's only agreed because the others did.'

Lucy was quiet as Garth said goodbye to the others and was thanked again for helping out. 'No, thanks for letting me join your family celebration. And such a great meal.'

'I'm sure it gets lonely over there for you. Now that Lucy and Liam are going to be here for a while, you'll have to come over more often. Make sure you come over before Seb and Jemmy head back, too.'

'I will.' He nodded with a smile as he held the door open for Lucy. 'I can walk home over the paddocks if you'd rather.'

Her smile was shy, different to the woman he'd made love to this morning.

'We'll take my car,' she said as they crossed the green lawn. He followed her to the machinery shed, where a small sedan was parked between the bales of hay.

As Lucy reached down to open the door, Garth swooped. He grabbed her around the waist and spun her around, backing her up against the hay bale as he nuzzled her neck. Satisfaction filled him as her arms laced around his neck, and she lifted her lips to his.

'God, I've wanted to kiss you all night.' He punctuated his words with kisses over her lips, her face, and her neck. Her deep, throaty chuckle sent a shiver through him, and he put his hands on either side of her face. 'And I want to tell you how happy I am that you're staying.'

'Whoa, boy.' Lucy stepped out of his arms and shook her head as she unlocked the car door. 'Don't get the wrong idea. I'm staying, but I'm not staying.'

Garth walked around to the other side of the car and opened the passenger door. 'Not staying?' Maybe old Harry was right.

'Three months on, three months back in Sydney and then three months back here. And then I'll go back to the city to stay for good.' She glanced at him as she started the car. 'I love what I do, and my career is going well. Goodbody and Grech is one of the top agencies in the country, and I'd be crazy to throw that away.'

Garth looked at Lucy as she backed the car out of the machinery shed and turned onto the road that led to the back gate between the two properties.

'I understand what you're saying. I love what I do, too. Now that I'm back home, that is.' The jolt that shot through his body when she turned briefly to him and held his eyes rattled him. Ever since he'd seen Lucy walking to the dam the other day, he hadn't been able to get her out of his head.

Hell, before Harry had shared his doubts, he'd even had crazy thoughts of her settling here and moving over with him and starting a brood of kids. He shook his head and looked away.

Slow down, man. She doesn't even want to stay out here in the Pilliga Scrub.

Garth jumped out as Lucy pulled up at the gate and opened it, waiting as she drove the car through to his property. 'I'll leave it open so you don't have to get out when you come back. There are no cattle in the back paddocks at the moment.'

The rest of the short drive was quiet, but tension hummed in the air between them. When they parked outside Garth's new house, Lucy climbed out of the car and followed him to the back door. Garth was surprised to see his hand shaking as he put the key in the lock. He held the door open as she stepped inside, and he reached for the light switch, but her hand caught his before he could flick it on.

'Leave them off.' Her voice was deep and throaty. God, he loved the sound of her voice and the beautiful smile he could see in the dim light. And it was for him.

He wanted her. And she stood there beside him, waiting, anticipating his move and he knew in a heartbeat that Lucy wanted him too.

He paused and dropped his forehead against hers as a tinge of sanity prevailed. 'Oh, God, Lucy. I just thought. We didn't use any protection last night.'

'It's all right, I'm on the pill.'

He stared at her, and her eyes were hazy with desire, and her voice was thick. Her heart was thudding against his chest as fast as his was. He smiled and pushed open the bedroom door.

##

Lucy shook her head a few hours later; Garth had led her to the bathroom off his bedroom and was running water in the huge tub.

'I'm sorry I haven't got any nice smelly stuff or bubbles. I only use the bath when my muscles are sore after a day on horseback.'

LUCY

'It's fine.' She watched as he pointed out the fluffy towels on the bench.

'Do you want someone to wash your back?' he asked with a smile.

'That would be nice, thank you.'

As she sat in the steaming hot water, Garth washed her back and massaged her neck muscles with firm fingers. 'Do you want to stay the night?'

'I'd love to, but we've got an early start in the morning, and now that Pop's home, Gran will need an extra hand with him, too.' Lucy shook her head reluctantly. 'But I will stay when it all settles down. 'If you want me to,' she said shyly.

'Of course I do.' Garth dried her off with a big fluffy towel, and they sat in the kitchen while Lucy's hair dried. She grinned at him. 'I know I'm going to get teased anyway, but I won't give them any ammunition.'

'You seem close to your cousins.' Garth's eyes were warm, and she looked down as he played with her fingers. 'I'll be honest, Lucy, I really like you being back here and close by.'

A strange feeling ran through Lucy. 'I'll be honest too. The idea of being here, out on the farm, isn't as bad as I thought it would be when Gran first mentioned it.' She looked at him as an unfamiliar shyness ran through her. 'And now we're . . . er . . . friends—' Heat tinged her cheeks as he grinned at her '—it will be fun. I mean, I won't have to put up with Liam's moods. If it gets too bad, I can always come over and visit you.'

'So, you and Liam first?'

'Yes, she nodded slowly. 'Me and Liam.'

CHAPTER 19

Six weeks later, Liam and Lucy had settled into a routine at Prickle Farm. Jemmy and Seb were back in the city but called every couple of days. Lucy listened with surprise as Liam outlined to Seb on the phone what he'd done that week. He hadn't been as moody as Lucy had expected, and she was happy with the way the work at Prickle Farm had been divided between them. Pop was recovering well and was getting around the property on one of the quad runners, albeit under Gran's eagle eye. Lucy was rarely needed out in the paddocks and she spent most of her days looking after the farmhouse and working on her current campaigns in between baking. Garth came over to help out when Liam needed a hand, and Liam had got into the habit of going over to Garth's place and helping out some afternoons. And no one had so much as raised an eyebrow at the number of nights that Lucy spent at Garth's.

On the second weekend after Seb and Jemima had gone back to Sydney, Lucy raided Gran's garden for cuttings.

'No, Lucy. That won't strike.' Gran tutted behind her. 'Come with me.'

Lucy followed Gran around to the back of the hay shed and stopped dead. A large fern house with an irrigation system spraying moisture onto rows and rows of potted plants lined the back of the large shed.

'Goodness, I didn't even know this was here.' Lucy stared in amazement.

Gran pointed to the middle shelf. 'Anything from there will grow in this soil as long as he keeps it watered and keeps the roos and rabbits away.' Gran pointed and Lucy followed the direction of her finger. 'These big pots are shrubs ready to plant. You can take as many as you like. Then I won't have to waste water on them.'

Lucy dropped a quick kiss on Gran's cheek before she took off at a run. 'You are a gem, Gran.'

'Where are you going now?'

'I'm going to get Pop's ute and load it up.'

##

A variety of plants, trees, and shrubs peeked over the top of the ute as Lucy drove slowly down the dirt road. She had loaded in as many of the plants as she could fit onto the tray. The padlock had been off the back gate since Gran had forgiven Garth, and it was now a short drive between the two properties. Garth was swinging the axe at the side of the woodshed. The mornings already had a tinge of crispness in the air, and the autumn winds had started to blow. A shaft of regret lodged in Lucy's chest. It would have been nice to sit by the fire with Garth on his soft sofa, but she would be back in Sydney in her cold and draughty apartment before winter set in. She stopped the car and watched, catching her breath at the sheer beauty of him as his muscles flexed and shimmered in the late afternoon sunlight. He swung the axe high, and a resounding crack echoed through the air as the log split. A pair of cut-off, frayed shorts revealed long, sinewy leg muscles. An expanse of bare chest met her eyes as her gaze travelled up to his shoulders. Her attention lingered on those broad shoulders, now glistening with perspiration. The reddish lights in his hair caught the sun, and his grin was wide when he turned to greet her.

He walked across to the ute, leaned in and kissed her mouth. 'Hello there, lovely Lucy.'

'Hello.' Lucy smiled up at him. 'I missed you this week.' She'd been in Sydney since Monday. Two trips down for the monthly meeting had kept her up to speed with her work, and with the internet connection at Garth's place, she was handling the telecommuting with ease.

'How was the trip to the big smoke?'

Lucy wondered why his tone was guarded. 'It was good. Caleb loves the way the campaign is shaping up.'

'That's good.' Garth opened the door for her, and after she climbed out, she took his hand and led him around to the back of the ute. 'What's all this?'

'I hope you dug the garden beds while I was away,' she said, sensing he didn't want to talk about her work. A glimmer of disquiet took away the pleasure of seeing him again. She filed that away to think about later.

'You asked me to dig the gardens, so of course I did.' His eyes widened as he looked in the back of the ute. 'But I don't think I dug enough to accommodate all of that.'

'Well, you're going to have to water these till they get planted.'

'Come and see what else I did.' He put his arm around her shoulders, and together, they walked around to the side of the house.

Lucy smiled as she looked at the work he had done around there. 'You have been working hard.'

A long row of garden beds edged the length of the house, and a medium-height fence ran along the edge of the pathway. A small wooden gate with an arch above it stood at the end near the back garden.

'Oh, that would be perfect for Gran's climbing rose.' Again, that glimmer of something tugged at her. 'Are you going to have time to look after all of this when I go back to Sydney, Garth? I know how busy you are with the farm.' Lucy moved away from his arm and walked up to the arch he had built over the gate.

His back was to the sun, and his eyes were shadowed. 'I guess I'll have to.'

For a moment, the silence was tense until Garth broke it with a laugh that sounded a bit forced. 'I don't want your gran coming over here and seeing dead plants. I'm still as scared of her as I was when I was a kid.'

'Come on, let's get these plants unloaded, and I'll water them.' Lucy followed him back to the ute, and they worked together unloading the plants and carrying them across to the shade in the hay shed. 'Where's the closest tap and hose?'

'I'll go and get it while you get the last of the pots from the ute.' She watched as he walked out of the shed. Honestly, she had to get over this need to look at him. She'd found herself daydreaming about Garth when she was at her desk in the city. She was letting herself get a bit too involved here. She turned her attention to the plants before she stood back with a grunt of satisfaction as she lined up the last pot in the row of shrubs. There were more than a hundred plants here, and it was too late to start planting them this afternoon. The sun was sinking quickly, and a beautiful pink sky was building over the western horizon. The contented mooing of the cattle in the paddock closest to the house filled the still afternoon air, and a couple of tiny birds chirped as they picked at the hayseed on the floor of the shed. A feeling of peace stole over her, and she pushed away the memory of the noisy city traffic that had bothered her more than usual this week.

As she mused, a couple of drops of water plopped onto her head. She swung around. Garth was holding the water hose, and his lips were stretched into a cheeky grin as he pointed the hose at her.

'Lucy love, you look really hot.'

She backed away as he stepped closer. 'Don't even think about it, Garth.' She squealed as the water arced towards her, catching the late afternoon sunlight in brilliant droplets. She wasn't quick enough; a soft mist of water drifted onto her hair and T-shirt.

'You are so in for it, Garth Mackenzie.'

Garth stood there for a moment before putting the hose down, a smile playing around his lips. He turned the tap off and strolled over to her, lifting her wet hair between his fingers and sliding his lips down her damp neck. Lucy shivered. She wasn't sure if it was from the water trickling down her back or the soft brushing of his lips on her skin.

'So how am I in for it, Luce?'

'You'll keep,' she said primly, but she couldn't stop the laugh bubbling up from her chest as he dropped his fingers to her wet T-shirt and began to peel it up slowly.

'Did you know they have a wet T-shirt competition at the B&S ball? You could enter it.'

Heat flooded her face and neck as she looked down at her T-shirt.

##

Garth frowned as he waited in the kitchen. Lucy had gone to the bathroom to dry off, knocking back his offer to get the towel for her. It was great to have her back, but for some reason, she was a little distant this afternoon. He'd managed to make her laugh but it hadn't been long before the serious look had come back into her eyes again. He didn't like the way it was making him feel. He gripped the edge of the kitchen bench top as he waited for the kettle to boil, staring out over the green paddocks. Winter was coming quickly, and that meant that Lucy's three months would be up, and she would be going back to the city full-time.

What did that mean for them? The speed at which their relationship was building was a problem. Not for him. He was delighted with them taking up where they had left off six years ago.

But he was destined for heartbreak. Lucy was going back to the city. No matter how much she did over at Prickle Creek Farm—the cooking, helping her grandmother in the garden—she was adamant that country life was a temporary thing for her. Helping out the family, that's all it was. And it looked like he was a bit of fun for her on the side.

What if I want more?

He remembered his thoughts a few weeks back when he'd considered that it might be time to take a wife.

They loved the same things. They both shared a passion for country and western music.

They watched movies together, argued politics, and both dreamed of holidays in the tropical north. On the nights Lucy stayed over, she seemed to enjoy pottering about his house and garden and soaking in the huge tub with him.

Seemed to. Maybe he was reading too much into it.

But she was a city person now. Although for the life of him, Garth couldn't understand how anyone could prefer living in Sydney to the outback. He knew the time Lucy was spending here with him was not going to change that. She didn't want to live out in the country. And he didn't want to live in the city. Each to his own, he thought, as disappointment shafted through him.

He couldn't change the way he was; he was a country boy, through and through. The city stifled him when he had to visit; he missed the golden paddocks of home, and he hated being in the crowded, noisy streets. Traffic blaring, car pollution, and a night sky where the stars were almost invisible.

Lucy wandered back through the hallway, running a comb through her wet hair.

'Luce?' He kept his voice even.

'Yes.' She paused in the doorway, and the knowledge that he was going to lose her soon was worse than a kick from an angry steer in the cattle crush.

'Tell me one thing you love about the city. One thing the country can't give you,' he asked.

'Is this a trick question?' Her voice was light.

'No. I'm trying to see what you love about it so much.'

She put the comb down on the countertop and tapped a finger to her chin. 'Well, I can get the best Thai food right next door to my apartment. And there's a great little Japanese restaurant around the corner,'

'That's two things,' he said. 'Don't you miss the stars?'

Lucy's tinkling laugh lodged in his heart like shards of glass. 'Come on, Garth. We have stars in the city, too!'

'Yeah, I guess you do.' He had no hope if the lure of the city was as trivial as a Thai restaurant.

He pulled himself out of his thoughts as the kettle whistled. 'You want a cuppa?'

God, how domesticated did that sound?

CHAPTER 20

The mad rush of cooking had finished at Prickle Creek Farm. Pop was on the mend and starting to get out and about on the quad bike more often, and Gran was spending more time in her garden. The only time Lucy saw Liam was on the nights when she was at Prickle Creek for dinner—and that wasn't very often. He spent all day out in the paddocks and most of the nights in the farm office with Pop. Lucy had watched him last night over dinner after she'd come back from Garth's place. She had been surprised when Garth said he had to go into town for a meeting. She'd assumed she would have dinner and spend the night there.

In the few weeks they had been here on the farm, Liam had toughened up. He looked like an outdoors, rugged man, and he'd lost the English pallor he'd had when he'd arrived. When he spoke to Pop, his face was animated, and his voice was full of enthusiasm. Lucy was surprised at how quickly he'd adapted to cattle work. She wondered what he'd do when their time was up, and Jemmy and Seb came out to take over.

She would be going back to the city and back to her job. Away from Garth and the Mackenzie Farm. It—whatever this thing was between them—had developed way too quickly. Lucy suspected it wouldn't be long before Garth asked her to stay or hinted at making their relationship permanent. She'd seen the way he looked at her when he didn't think she was watching. It drove a spike of pain right through her. She couldn't stay here. There was no future for them. He was firmly entrenched in the land and his property. She had her career and was a part of the city, and that's where she wanted to be.

It was.

It was time to pull back and put some space between them. Gran had baked some scones, wrapped them in a tea towel and told Lucy to take them over to Garth. Despite her best intentions, it didn't take much persuasion for her to get into the car and drive over. No matter what her city girl brain told her, her heart won out. She wanted to see him.

As Lucy drove over the third cattle grid after going through the gate, she glanced to the west. Garth's horse was tethered to the fence that formed the eastern border between the two properties. Lucy pulled over to the side of the

LUCY

dusty road and put her hand up to her eyes, squinting in the strong afternoon sun. Garth was about fifty metres along the fence, and as she walked towards him, he leaned back and pulled the wire tight. She reached up and shooed the small black flies that always aimed unerringly for her eyes. His muscles strained beneath the tight T-shirt, and his hat was tipped forward over his eyes as he concentrated on tightening the fence wire. His head was down, and Lucy gasped as a movement in the red dirt behind him caught her attention.

A large snake was slithering towards his legs. Lucy stopped walking and put her hand over her mouth. If she called out or caught Garth's attention as she got closer, he was likely to step back and land right on it.

A six-foot eastern brown snake. One of the deadliest in the west. Perspiration ran down her face, and the flies were forgotten as she stood and watched. The snake came to a stop about a metre behind Garth's legs, but she knew how quickly they could strike. Her heart thudded, and dread filled her chest.

Oh, no. What should she do? Before she could move, Garth's cattle dog began to bark and ran between Garth and the snake. The snake reared and struck the dog as Lucy screamed. 'Run forwards, Garth! Snake!'

Garth dropped the wire strainer and, with one hand on the wire, vaulted over the fence in one fluid movement as the dog barked and circled around the snake.

'Stay there, Luce,' he called. 'I've got a whip on my saddle.'

As she watched, he ran along the fence to the shade where his horse was tethered and pulled his stock whip off the pommel of the saddle. He whistled to the dog to come as he approached the fence. Jack, his red kelpie, limped over to Garth and flopped into the dirt as he cracked the whip and the snake twirled in the air.

Lucy ran over to Garth, and he put one arm around her shoulder. 'Thanks, Luce. That bugger snuck up on me.'

'Garth.' Lucy gulped in a breath. 'I think it bit Jack before you got it.'

He leaned down to the small red dog panting on the hot ground, his eyes cloudy.

'Hell, I think the bloody thing did.' Garth looked around. 'Damn. I knew I should have brought the ute out.'

'What do you need to do?'

'I need to keep him still and get him into town to the vet.' As he spoke, Jack started to twitch and his muscles went into a spasm. 'I wonder where it got him.'

'On his back leg, I think,' Lucy said. 'Pick him up. I'll drive you into town.'

'Thanks, sweetheart.'

The endearment hit her like a punch to her chest. Garth was unaware of her inner turmoil as he lifted the dog and ran to Lucy's car. She grabbed a blanket from the boot and spread it on the back seat and he gently laid the small dog on it as she jumped behind the wheel.

***

Garth sat in the back with the dog cradled gently in his large hands and spoke softly to Jack as Lucy sped back into Prickle Creek.

'If you want to tell the vet we're on the way, my phone's in my bag on the floor,' Lucy spoke over her shoulder as they got closer to town, where the mobile phone service kicked in.

Garth made the call and kept one hand on Jack's forehead. Jack was his best dog and was more than a work dog; he was old, and he'd had him before he'd gone away to the west. He clenched his jaw as Lucy accelerated; she knew Jack was special to him.

By the time they pulled up outside the vet's surgery, Rod, the local veterinarian, was waiting for them with the antivenene loaded and ready to inject.

'I'll put him on oxygen too,' he said as Jack lay on the stainless-steel table. Rod looked up from the dog and smiled at Lucy. 'Hello, Lucy, I heard you were back in town.'

Garth pushed away the surge of jealousy that ripped through him when Lucy bestowed a high-wattage smile on the good-looking vet.

'Oh hi, Rod, I'm so sorry, all my attention was on Jack. I didn't even realise it was you. You came back to Prickle Creek?'

'As soon as I qualified.' Rod glanced across at Garth before he turned to Lucy. 'You've moved back too?'

'Oh no, I'm only visiting.'

'How about coming to dinner on the weekend, and you can tell me what you've been up to.'

'I'd like that.' Lucy's voice was strange, and she looked away from Garth as she accepted the invitation. 'It'll be great to catch up.'

Disbelief slammed through Garth as Lucy flirted with Rod, and he tightened his lips. Maybe she could have said, 'we'd like that,' or 'we could both come.' She could have given the guy an indication that she was in a relationship. He frowned; at least, he thought they were. It was time to talk about what Lucy thought and what she wanted.

##

'Good to see Rod working back in town,' Lucy said as they headed back home.

'Yes.' Garth looked away and watched the brown paddocks flash past.

'I sat next to him right through primary school.'

'Did you?' Garth said.

'He always wanted to be a vet. Good to see he got there.'

'Yes.' The word was almost a grunt, but Garth didn't particularly want to talk about Rod Rogers.

'He said Jack would be okay, so don't be too upset. He'll be fine.' This time, her smile was tentative.

'Yep.'

Lucy shot him a funny look, but he turned to stare out the window again.

'I'm really surprised that he came back to Prickle Creek,' she said.

This time, he couldn't help himself. 'And why's that, Lucy? Because it's not a place that anyone with any brains would want to live? Have you ever thought that's only your opinion of the place? Some of us love living out here. Give me the west over the city any day.'

'What are you so angry about?'

The hurt in her voice calmed Garth a little bit. 'Lucy, what do you want?'

She shot him a funny look, but he turned to stare out the window again. 'What do you mean, what do I want?'

'What do you want out of life? Do you want a career? Do you want to stay in the city?'

'I made my intentions quite clear when I first came to your place, if you think back, Garth. You said you agreed.' Her response was clipped and Garth noticed her hands tighten on the steering wheel.

'I guess you did.' He slunk down in the seat and tipped his head back.

I've got no chance of changing her mind.

The rest of the trip home was quiet, and he pointed to the paddock where he'd left his horse beneath the trees. 'Just drop me here, please.'

'See you later, maybe.' Her voice was quiet.

'Maybe.' Garth watched as the dust billowed behind the car as she drove towards Prickle Creek Farm.

Okay, so they were sleeping together, and maybe he'd been stupid to think it meant anything, but he'd not been able to stop his dream of making a life with Lucy. Out here in the country. Like she said, she'd told him at the outset what her intentions were. The more time she'd spent with him over the past six weeks, the deeper and harder he'd fallen for her. She had seemed to enjoy working with him, getting the garden in order, cooking meals with him, and just being together. Foolishly, he'd thought that meant she'd softened in her attitude about being back out here in the Pilliga.

They could sit in the living room at night and not speak for an hour, and the silence was comfortable. How stupid was he to think that meant she wanted to stay?

How stupid had he been to start that argument in the car? The bloody green-eyed monster of jealousy had pushed him into it. Rod was an old school friend, but it had fired up his insecurity. He wasn't good enough for Lucy; he didn't measure up to what she wanted in life. How stupid was he to think she'd be happy as a farmer's wife? Because that's the direction his thoughts had been taking.

Garth bit his lip as he walked towards his horse.

He'd built up a dream of what he thought would happen. But what was that saying?

It takes two to tango.

Because she would go back to the city. He was kidding himself. He was just a nice little sideline for her while she was here.

Filling in her nights. Flirting. Sleeping with him. A toy boy. Garth slammed his fist into his palm, and his horse jumped as he approached.

'Sorry, Brownie.'

He knew he was being unfair, but the thought of Lucy leaving left him cold and empty.

All along, she'd been upfront about going back to the city, but foolishly, he'd thought he could entice her to stay. He was the fool. How could you fight something like that?

He kicked at the dirt as he led Brownie past the dead snake and over to the gate. The snake was black and covered with ants, and he stood there staring at it for a moment. Maybe it was time for a wake-up call.

LUCY

CHAPTER 21

Lucy closed her eyes and squeezed back the tears as she drove back to the main road to Prickle Farm. Regret sat in her throat like a brick. Why couldn't Garth understand how she felt? How many times had she tried to tell him she was not going to stay?

She'd known straight away that he'd been hurt when she hadn't included him when she and Rod had discussed catching up. She should have turned to him and said, 'How about it, Garth?' but that would have been publicly outing them as a couple. And they weren't. And she didn't want them to be.

Did she?

Oh, hell, I don't know what I want.

The look on Garth's face and the tightness of his lips as they'd driven out of town had shown her how much she'd hurt him with her hastily thought-up response.

Stupid, stupid. Why hadn't she just sat him down and told him how it was going to be?

Because I don't think I can. Maybe this was the best way. Let him think she was fickle. Let him be the one to pull back because he was hurt.

Because he didn't trust her anymore. Maybe now, he'd believe that she was serious about going back to the city. Maybe he'd realise that there was no future for them.

He was country.

She was city.

And his words when he'd lashed out at her had shown her that in bucket loads. They were totally incompatible. Okay, so they were perfect together—they enjoyed each other's company, and they had so much in common.

Lucy shook her head as she slammed the car door in the hay shed. She was going to have to forget all about Garth McKenzie and move on. It would be a lot easier when she was back in Sydney, and it was time to do something about that.

Gran and Pop were out visiting a neighbour, and Liam looked at her curiously as she clomped up the back steps.

'Everything okay? Good trip? How was Sydney?'

'No.' She choked back a sob. 'I had to take Garth to town the other day. Jack got bitten by a brown snake in the front paddock.' Hopefully, Liam would think she was upset about the dog.

LUCY

She was, but Rod had assured them Jack would survive.

'Gran and Pop rang; they're going to stay out for dinner. Are you going to Garth's?' Liam followed her up the steps to the verandah that went around the whole house.

'No. I'm tired, and I'm not hungry. I'm going to have an early night.'

He laughed. 'I was sure you'd be over there again tonight. You haven't seen him much in the past week.'

Lucy whirled around, and Liam bore the brunt of the feelings that were surging through her. 'Well, I'm not, and I wish you would all stop assuming we're a couple. We're not, and I'm going back to Sydney in six weeks. Remember?'

Her face crumpled, and she burst into tears.

'Hey, Luce.' Liam's hand on her arm stopped her from opening the door and running inside. 'What's wrong? Really?'

Lucy's shoulders sagged, and Liam pushed open the door and held it open for her. 'Come and sit down and tell me what's wrong. I'll get us a cold drink.'

Lucy flopped onto the soft lounge and lifted her face up to the cool air puffing out of the air-conditioner. She was pleased that Gran and Pop were out. At least there was only Liam to see her have a meltdown.

He walked from the kitchen and handed her a glass of juice with ice cubes chinking in it.

'So spill. You obviously need a shoulder to cry on. Did you and Garth have a blue?' Liam pulled up a wooden chair and sat in front of her. Lucy grinned through her tears. His face was grimy and there was a line of red dirt where his hat had caught the perspiration as he'd worked out in the hot paddocks all day. He totally looked the part of a cattleman.

'You've really taken to country life, haven't you,' she said.

'You have, too. You've fit in so well you could join the Country Women's Association and enter their bake-offs.' Liam tried to jolly her along. 'I'm sure you'd win a prize for your cakes at the agricultural show. It's on the weekend after next.'

She shook her head, and her lip quivered. 'But that's not what I want to do.'

Liam leaned forward and took her hand. 'Is that the problem? You don't know what you want?'

'Oh, I know what I want.' Lucy's smile was bitter. 'I want Garth. But I don't want to live out here. And I can't have one without the other.'

'Very true.' Liam nodded. 'Take care that you make the right decision, Lucy. I made the wrong one a few years back, and I've regretted it ever since.'

'What happened?' Lucy stared at him. 'That's if you want to share.'

'Water under the bridge now. I can talk about it without it hurting too badly.' His voice was sad, and she stared at him.

'I fell in love with an Aussie girl I met in London. Angie's work visa ran out, and she had to come back to Australia.'

'And?'

'She wanted me to come back with her, but foolishly, I put my career first. It was before the first round of job cuts in Fleet Street, and of course, I planned on being the next Clive James.' He lifted his head, and his eyes were bleak. 'Too late, I realised I shouldn't have let Angie go.' His laugh was bitter. 'And the irony? I'm back here now, my journalism career's over, and I'm making a new life she would have loved.' He shook his head. 'She's a country girl, and she was doing a vet exchange just outside of London.'

'Can't you get in touch and let her know you're home?' Lucy frowned. It all sounded so simple when it was someone else's problem.

'Nope. Too much pride. Last time she emailed me, she had a new man and was living happily in Victoria. She doesn't need to know I've come home. No point.'

'I think you should.' Her voice was emphatic.

'We're as different as chalk and cheese. I'll let her be. She's found her happy place. But what about you? We all have opinions about other people's lives, Lucy. I think you should give Garth a chance. You obviously love him, and he loves you. Have you told each other that, or do you skirt around it like Angie and I did?' Liam shook his head again and lifted his glass. 'Does it really matter where you live if you love somebody? Think about it, Lucy.'

As he held her eyes, Lucy could see the sadness in their depths and that stayed with her when she went to bed. She tossed and turned as she thought about what Liam had said. But his well-meaning advice didn't change her mind. A few minutes before the lights of Gran and Pop's

LUCY

Lexus flashed through her window, she heard Liam's truck start up and wondered where he was going. She climbed out of bed and slipped a pair of loose, long pants over her pyjamas.

'Hey, Luce. You're up late.' Pop was almost as sprightly as he had been years before. He crossed the kitchen and picked up the electric jug. 'Cuppa?'

'Yes, please. Where did Liam go?'

'He went to turn the irrigator off. He's a good lad,' Pop said.

'Everything okay, love?' Gran patted her hand as she sat at the table beside her while Pop rattled around the cupboards reaching for cups and saucers as the jug came to the boil.

'Gran, I have a huge favour to ask.' Lucy managed to keep her voice steady.

'Anything, pet.' She looked up at Pop as he took the milk from the fridge. 'Harry, there's some of that cheesecake lattice slice in a Tupperware container on the bottom shelf. I think Lucy needs some cheering up.'

Lucy waited until Pop joined them at the table, and Gran pushed the sweet, creamy slice over to her. Lucy shook her head. 'No, thanks. I'm putting on weight with all this country cooking. My clothes are getting tight. Too much good food and not enough exercise.'

'Well, I'm having some.' Pop picked up a piece of the slice and smiled at her as he chewed. 'So what's the favour?'

'I know we changed the conditions of what Gran had asked for originally and said we would stay for three months and then come back after the others had their turn, but I need to go back to Sydney.' She rushed on quickly. 'I need to go back and do some work. I'll come back later in the year, and I'll stay longer after Jemmy and Seb go back.'

Pop and Gran exchanged a knowing look.

'You really don't need me here at the moment. The harvest is almost over. All I'm doing is cooking and filling cake tins and helping'—she picked up her cup and took a sip of tea as her voice threatened to break—'and helping Garth get his garden in order. And that wasn't really part of the deal, and I'm not pulling my weight anyhow, and you really won't—'

'Lucy.' Gran's voice was firm, and she took Lucy's hand. 'You can do whatever you want. We're not going to hold you to that silly idea I had. I was so worried none of you would want the farm. I was too hard on you all by setting conditions. Pop and I know you all want to keep the place, and whatever happens, we'll work it out. You have your own life, and you have commitments.'

Tears filled Lucy's eyes. 'Oh, Gran, really?'

'Really. We're together again as a family, and I hope that we won't go back to the way we all were. No matter what happens here or where you all end up.' Gran looked at her with shrewd eyes. 'Although I must say I'm surprised. I really thought Jemmy would be the one to go. I thought Garth Mackenzie would keep you here.'

Lucy dropped her head to hide the sadness she knew was in her eyes. 'No, we're incompatible; we want different things out of life.'

Gran took Lucy's hand and rubbed her thumb along her skin. 'Are you sure, Lucy? That boy loves you. I know he does.'

Lucy's throat closed, and she shook her head, waiting until she got control of her voice again. 'Yes, I'm sure. We've had fun, but Garth would want things his own way in the long run. It's easier for me to go back sooner than later.'

The back door opened, and Liam's voice drifted through as he yelled at the dogs. Lucy and Gran exchanged a smile. Liam had settled onto the farm as though he'd been born to do it. He walked in and looked around.

'Yum, lattice slice.' He reached out, and Gran slapped his hand away.

'Go and wash your hands, Liam. I shouldn't have to tell you. You're too big for that.'

'Irrigator all sorted?' Pop looked at him curiously. 'You were a while.'

'One of the grain trucks had a flat, so I helped them change it.'

Lucy leaned back in her chair and watched as Liam left his boots by the door and headed into the laundry adjacent to the kitchen. As he walked back into the kitchen, his broad smile turned into a frown. 'This looks serious? Have I missed another family talk?'

'Lucy is going back to the city a bit early,' Gran said with a smile. 'Her employers need her, and we're all good here.'

Liam's gaze was shrewd. 'So that's why you're running away, Luce? Your employers want you?'

She could hear the disappointment in his voice, and Gran looked at them both with curiosity as Lucy snapped back at him. 'Don't judge me by your experiences, okay?' She shoved her chair back. 'I'm going to bed.

Goodnight.' She strode to the door and then paused and turned back to the table, dropping a kiss on Pop's bald head and hugging Gran.

'Night, you pair.'

She knew Liam's eyes were on her, and she didn't care. It was the only decision she could make. Garth's attitude this afternoon had given her the opportunity to pull back.

It was time to do what she had wanted to all along.

CHAPTER 22

Once you made a decision, there was no point hanging around. Lucy looked around the room as she shoved her clothes into her bag. In the time she'd been here, she'd settled in, and it was going to be lonely going back to her apartment in Newtown, but it wouldn't take long to get back into her old routine. And the bonus was that Seb and Jemmy were in town until they came back here, so she would still have family around her.

'Lucy, telephone!' Gran called down the hallway as Lucy was in the bathroom getting her toiletries.

Her stomach tightened, and nausea actually skittered up into her throat.

Garth.

She didn't want to leave on bad terms, but she wasn't ready to talk to him yet. She'd go and find him in the paddocks before she left.

'Tell Garth I'll call in and see him later, please, Gran.'

'It's not Garth; it's Rod from the vet in Spring Downs.'

LUCY

Lucy hurried down the hallway, worried that Jack had had a relapse after his snake bite. She took the phone from Gran. 'Hi, Rod. Is everything okay? I was going to call you later.' She crossed her fingers behind her back; she'd totally forgotten about having dinner with him on Saturday night.

'Yes, all good here, Lucy. Listen, something's come up on the weekend, and I can't make dinner. We're having a quiet day on the surgery because of the agricultural show up in Coonamble. Half the town's gone up there. I was wondering if you were coming into town at all. I have some news for you and wanted to catch up.'

'I'm actually going back to Sydney today, but I could call in and see you on the way.' Lucy turned away, aware that Gran was standing next to her, ears flapping and her lips pursed.

'What time are you leaving?' Rod asked.

'I'll be getting away in the next couple of hours, so I'll be in town around lunchtime.'

'How about I meet you at the R.S.L. club for lunch? It's cool there, and they don't do a bad meal. You have to eat if you've got that long trip ahead of you.'

'Sounds good. See you then.'

Lucy walked past Gran without satisfying her obvious curiosity.

##

The farewell with Gran and Pop a little while later was hard.

Pop whispered into her hair as he held her close. 'Love you, Lucy. And promise you'll be back soon, okay?'

'I promise.' Lucy held out her arms to Gran and hugged her. 'Love you too, Gran.'

Gran reached up and wiped away a tear, but it was a happy one. 'Get away with you. Enough of this lovey-dovey talk.' But she held Lucy close for a minute before she let her go.

Liam was out in the hay shed as Lucy carried her bags to the car. Gran and Pop stood on the top step.

'I'm going now,' she said.

'I can see that.' Liam's gaze dropped to her bag. Lucy had loaded the rest of her stuff, including her computer, into the car earlier.

'You're going to see Garth, I hope?' he said quietly as he lifted a load of hay onto the back of the truck next to the cattle salt blocks.

Lucy bit back the retort that sprang to her lips and huffed a patient sigh. 'Yes, Liam. I'm going to see him on the way out.'

LUCY

She leaned over and kissed his cheek, but before she could step back, he held her arm.

'Lucy, be very, very sure you are doing the right thing. I would hate to see you hurt.'

'I will. I haven't made any decisions. I'm going back to the city to think about it.' Her words surprised her, but it was the truth.

Not that there was anything to make a decision about. They'd had a relationship, but there'd been no talk of commitment. Just an acceptance that she was city, he was country.

'I have to get going; I'm meeting someone in town for lunch.'

Liam nodded and turned back to the truck. 'Make sure you ring us when you get home.'

'I will.' Lucy smiled at him. 'And thanks, Liam. It's good to have you back in my life.'

She opened the car door and started the engine, waving to Gran and Pop as she drove slowly past the house. The road out to Spring Downs was dry, and red dust flew behind her as she accelerated towards the turn-off. As the gate of the Mackenzie farm appeared in the distance, Garth's Land Cruiser ute turned onto the Coonamble Road ahead of her.

Damn, I should have called. She tried to keep up with him to see where he turned off so she could follow him to stop and say goodbye, but his ute roared ahead, and she couldn't keep up. Gradually, the white ute disappeared over the crest of a hill and by the time she reached it, there was no sign of him ahead. There were a couple of tracks leading to the back of the large Mackenzie property, and Lucy slowed her car. There was no dust hanging in the air. Garth must be heading into town. She'd try and track him down there. It wouldn't be hard. A bank, a newsagent, a garage, a produce store, the milk bar and the R.S.L. comprised the whole business area. There wouldn't be many places to look.

By the time she approached the fifty-kilometre zone at the edge of Prickle Creek, it was almost noon. She drove slowly down the main street, looking for Garth's ute, but there was no sign of it. Guilt trickled through her. She hated leaving without saying goodbye. There was only one thing for it: she would call him from Sydney and have a good frank talk about how she felt.

Lucy shook her head as she parked in the R.S.L. car park. Maybe if she waited for half an hour or so, Garth would turn up in town.

Rod was waiting for her in the bistro, a huge jug of iced water in the middle of the table. He stood as she crossed the empty restaurant to join him. He took her hand, leaned over and kissed her cheek.

'I'm so pleased you had time to stop on your way back to Sydney.' He pulled out her chair for her, and she sat down. 'A shopping trip?'

'No, I'm going home.'

'Home? I thought you'd moved out here.' Rod frowned as he poured a glass of water, and the ice cubes tinkled as they filled her glass. 'I thought you and Garth were together?'

'No.' Lucy surprised herself with her calm response. 'I'm going back to Sydney to my job.'

As they chatted over lunch, Lucy kept a close eye on the car park. But there was no sign of Grant. Her heart closed down more as every minute passed.

'It was great to catch up, Rod, even briefly,' she said as she stood to leave.

'Make sure you keep in touch when you come back again. I'd love you to meet Laura, my fiancée.'

'I won't be back.' Even to her own ears, her voice was flat. Lucy walked slowly across the hot bitumen to her car. It was time to leave. Far away from the files, and the dust and the prickles

. . . and Garth Mackenzie and the attraction that had settled into her heart.

CHAPTER 23

Lucy stood on the corner of King Street and Enmore Road, waiting for the pedestrian light to change to red. She was on her way up to the Enmore Theatre to meet with the director about some flyers for the upcoming production of *Hamlet*. The traffic roared past along the busy road to her right, and the roar of the trains mingled with the sounds of the cars in sensory overload. She closed her eyes and opened them straight away as someone jostled her from behind and almost pushed her into the traffic speeding past.

'Watch it,' she snapped. But the guy had his phone glued to his ear and didn't even acknowledge her warning.

The traffic fumes mingled with the greasy smell of the McDonalds on the corner, and she put her hand to her mouth as her stomach roiled. Ever since she'd come back to Sydney, her stomach had been sensitive, and she'd been Googling water parasites, convinced she'd picked up a bug or something in the dam at Prickle Farm. The light changed, and Lucy stepped out with the crowd of people to hurry across the road. Horns blared and water splashed up her legs as a motorbike rider wove his bike illegally through the red light and hit a puddle as he passed her.

'Moron.' She shook her fist, shaken by the near miss. She reached the footpath and turned left, heading for the theatre. As she passed the Turkish pizza place a few shops along, her stomach churned as the strong smell of garbage from the bin on the footpath reached her. She stepped out onto the road to avoid the overflow of empty cups, rolled-up papers and pizza crusts. Another horn blared, and she jumped back onto the footpath, her irritation growing by the minute. Since she'd been away, the city had got filthy. And noisy. And smelly. And there seemed to be many more people on the streets.

A couple of schoolgirls ran past and giggled as Lucy stood staring at the garbage on the ground.

She pulled her water bottle from her backpack and took a swig, trying to calm herself.

Lucy sighed as she turned into the foyer of the theatre. She'd been back at work three weeks, and her motivation was non-existent. Seb had tried to get out of her what was wrong, but she wouldn't be led down that path.

'Just the weather,' she'd said when he told her she was looking peaky. He'd been surprised when she'd bowled into the office as soon as she came back from the farm, and he was full of excitement about his upcoming stay out west. He was sitting on the chair in her cubby hole when she came back from the theatre and threw her bag on the bench that ran along the wall.

'Bloody traffic is horrendous today,' she muttered.

'You're in a good mood.' He narrowed his eyes and looked her up and down. Trying to make herself feel better, Lucy had dressed in her high boots and skin-tight yellow leggings. Her pink T-shirt had a series of bright red lips all over it in various shapes and sizes.

'You look like crap.'

'That's how I feel.' Lucy pushed her hair back from her face. Her fringe had grown, and she didn't even have the motivation to make a hair appointment. 'It's just so hot and noisy and dirty here.'

'It's no different to when you left,' Seb told her on the phone one night. 'Are you sure it's not because you're pining for Prickle Creek?'

'No.' Her voice was terse, and she scowled. 'Of course not.'

Seb's voice was soft. 'Liam and I were talking last night.'

Lucy's head flew up.

'He said you've barely talked to Gran and Pop since you rang to say you were back in Sydney safe and sound.'

'No need,' she said shortly.

'He said Garth was asking after you yesterday.'

'That's nice,' she said as she stared across the room.

'Aren't you in touch with him either? I thought you were great mates.'

'No, I'm busy. Gran's quite happy with the way things worked out, so I don't need to live in their pocket. Or Garth's. I'm back into my life now.'

'It would still be nice to keep in touch with them.'

'I haven't given Garth a thought since I left. Why would I?

'Maybe because you care about each other?'

'Huh. Maybe not.' Lucy folded her arms as irritation flooded her. 'But even if we did, it could never work out. Can you see Garth living here in the city? Can you see me living out there in the red dust? I love this city. And there are no flies, or prickles or smelly cows. It's got everything that I want.'

'Like what?' Seb's relentless questioning was getting to her.

'Like . . . like a Thai restaurant.'

'Yeah, that's a really important thing to have.'

'All right. I'll ring tonight. Now, if you don't mind, I've got some flyers to knock out for the theatre.'

'Whatever happened to the advertising campaign for the lingerie firm? The photos I took of Garth?'

'They decided to go with beach shots instead.' Lucy's voice was short. She wasn't going to tell Seb she was glad about Caleb's decision because it meant that Garth wouldn't have to come to the city. That would have interfered with her getting over him. The getting over that wasn't happening. She'd soaked her pillowcase every night as she tried to figure out what was wrong with her. She didn't want to be at the farm, but the longer she was in Sydney, she realised she didn't want to be here either. Garth was a part of her, and she missed him like crazy.

He could have called to see how she was. But he hadn't, so obviously he wasn't missing her.

'Fair enough. Listen, Gran's hoping *everyone* will be home for the long weekend in June.' Seb stared at her, and Lucy lifted her chin. 'Jemmy and I are going. We could travel home together. It's only a couple of weeks after that that we move out there for your turn.'

'It's not home,' Lucy cried. 'Not for me!'

'It is for some of us, as strange as it may seem. Think about it. Why don't you come with us? I'll take my ute instead of the bike.'

'What ute?' Lucy sniffed and wiped the back of her hand over her eyes.

'The ute I bought for when I go up there to stay.'

'Stay?'

Sebastian's voice was firm. 'When I go, I'm staying there for good. I'm leaving the city. Liam and I have already talked about sharing the work. I think you need to know that. He's talking about staying on past his three months.'

Lucy shook her head in disbelief. Was everyone deserting her?

The day was long, and Lucy was busy with three new projects. Caleb was throwing a lot of work her way and was hinting at a permanent job.

LUCY

On the way home, Lucy stopped at her favourite Thai restaurant just up the road from her apartment. For the first time in weeks, she was starving. Maybe she was finally getting used to being back. She waited for her order and carried it home. As soon as she opened the door, she threw her work bag and laptop on the couch and grabbed a fork. She was ravenous and didn't even bother with a plate.

She sat back on the sofa when she finished feeling as though she was about to explode,

It was time to pull up her big girl panties, concentrate on her work, and forget about Garth Mackenzie. A movie and a good night's sleep were all she needed. Tomorrow would be a new beginning.

She might even ring Gran and think about going back to Prickle Creek Farm for the long weekend. Maybe, just maybe.

Three hours after the movie finished, Lucy lay in bed in her small bedroom in Newtown, listening to the never-ceasing roar of the traffic. Where were so many people going at three a.m.? She rolled over and punched her pillow as the blare of a siren drifted through the open window. Even though she was tired, she hadn't been able to sleep. She closed her eyes and visualised the quiet paddocks at Prickle Farm; the problem was every time she got the quiet scene embedded into her thoughts, Garth Mackenzie strode into the picture. And then, of course, the picture moved to his house.

They'd cooked meals together; she'd hung a couple of prints that he'd not had time to put up, and she'd put some feminine touches around the place. She'd even filled his freezer with homemade goodies for him, although they would have run out by now. He was probably back on bought biscuits unless Gran had taken pity on him.

Lucy sat up and put her hands over her eyes. The way they'd said goodbye had been awful. She needed closure so she could move on with her life and forget about Garth. When she'd left, she'd been certain that the city was what she wanted,

And back then, all she'd wanted to do was come back to Sydney. The last three weeks had been an eye-opener for her. Why hadn't the noise and the crowds bothered her before she went home to Prickle Creek Farm? What had happened to her out there to make her notice the frantic pace of the city now? The traffic and the noise, which she'd never noticed before, contrasted so much with the silence of the farm; she closed her eyes and longed for the serenity of the bush. How come she hadn't noticed everyone scurrying around intent on their lives, with no time for conversation? The one time she'd tried to strike up a personal conversation with the boss, Caleb had stood there in his black jeans and T-shirt and looked at her as though she'd suddenly grown two heads.

She'd been a cow to get on with at work, and she owed Seb an apology or three for how short she'd been with him. Not only in personal conversations but when they'd been out on a couple of photo shoots together, too. Maybe it was time she admitted to herself that she loved Prickle Creek Farm.

Almost as much as she loved Garth Mackenzie.

Lucy let a smile cross her face as she came to a decision. It was time to go home.

CHAPTER 24

Garth pushed the gate closed behind Liam and Seb as they led the last of the straggling cattle into the back paddock. Seb had come up from Sydney for the weekend. 'Thanks, Liam. Appreciate the help, Seb.' He lifted his hat and wiped the sweat off his brow. Even though they'd left moving the cattle until late afternoon, the heat rose off the dry, parched earth in shimmering waves. The cattle gathered immediately around the dam, and Liam nodded slowly.

'That looks like a damn fine idea to me. Want me to grab some beers, and we'll meet you down at the back dam for a swim?' he said.

Garth shook his head. 'Got some things I need to do. I'll take a rain check.'

He was aware of Liam and Seb's quiet conversation as he called Jack and strode over to his ute parked on the other side of the fence. He was grateful for the help that the guys were giving him lately, but he found it too hard to spend time in their company. He'd lost count of the number of times he'd knocked back Helena and Harry's invitation to come over for a meal.

LUCY

Garth clenched his jaw as he started the ute. He couldn't get damn Lucy Peterkin out of his head, no matter where he went. He was surprised she hadn't even come home for the long weekend. As he drove along the track, he wondered how the hell he could get her out of his head once and for all.

It was time to make a move, or he'd be mooning about for the rest of his life. The property was suffering, the house was a mess, and his emotions weren't much better. He'd been wrong, and it was time to go and see Lucy and sort it once and for all.

He missed her like hell, but he had to get over the fact that she didn't want him.

Garth threw his work boots into the laundry, and they landed with a satisfying thud. Seb and Liam hadn't mentioned Lucy once today. Something was going on.

But it's none of my business.

He headed for the shower, stripped off his filthy work clothes, and threw them on the floor. Every damn room in his house had a memory of Lucy. Sometimes, he thought he was losing his mind. She filled his thoughts no matter what he was doing. He'd spent more time in the garden trying to get her out of his mind, but every time he turned the hose on, a picture of her in one of her silly T-shirts replaced the view in front of him.

He stood under the hot water, letting it wash away the dirt and soothe his feelings. He'd fallen for Lucy, but she'd made it quite clear from the outset that she wouldn't stay.

More fool him; he hadn't listened. Now, Garth forced himself to step back and think about what he really wanted. Was it being here on the farm and living out in the Pilliga Scrub? How important was that to his future? He had enough money in the bank to start afresh. He could put a manager in if need be.

Where did he want to be? Could he be happy if he stayed here without Lucy?

A resounding no crashed through his thoughts.

Garth thought of the nights Lucy had spent in his bed and the fun they'd had working in his garden. The joy on her face as she'd planted the tiny seedlings and watched them take root in the soil. The feeling that had filled him when he'd held her in his arms.

Garth accepted he didn't want to be here without Lucy. The farm was nothing without her.

LUCY

Maybe she could love him if they were where she wanted to be. In the city, where she could work in the career she loved. There were plenty of engineering opportunities in Sydney, and he had a lot of contacts. He'd have no problem finding a job.

Knowing he'd hurt Lucy when he'd fought with her in the car the day the snake had bitten Jack, sent regret spiralling through him.

Garth turned the shower jets off and reached for a towel. He crossed to the window, and as he stood staring out at the paddocks, he came to a decision.

He loved Lucy Peterkin, and he would do anything to keep her. If she wanted him. That's what he had to find out.

No matter what it took. No matter where he had to live. No matter what he had to lose, nothing was as bad as losing her.

***

Liam and Seb shared a satisfied look when Garth turned up at the dam with a six-pack and a request for them to keep an eye out on the property while he went to Sydney to see Lucy.

'She's bloody miserable, mate,' Liam said as he took the beer that Garth held out.

Garth quirked an eyebrow. 'So she talks to you lot?'

'Gran called her the other night and wouldn't take any excuse about why she couldn't talk,' Seb added with a frown. 'I don't think she's doing too well back in the city, is our Lucy. The last time I saw her at the office, she was complaining about the traffic and the noise.'

'And too stubborn to admit she's wrong. So don't give up too easily.' Liam looked pleased when he heard that Garth was leaving first thing in the morning.

'She's been at the office every day for three weeks, keeping herself busy,' Seb said with a frown. 'But she did seem cranky when I said I was coming up for the weekend.'

'Persevere, mate.' Liam lay back, and his voice was soft as it floated over the water. 'I'll bet twenty bucks that she'll come back home with you.'

'I wish I was so sure.' Garth stared into the distance as the setting sun sent a flare of purple into the evening sky. His future depended on it. If Lucy didn't want him he didn't know what he'd do with his life.

***

LUCY

At sunset the following day, Garth stood in the narrow foyer of an old apartment block at the back of King Street, Newtown. He wrinkled his nose as the sour smell of beer-soaked carpet and mould assailed him. Seb had warned him that Lucy's apartment was in a dodgy part of Newtown when he'd called him for her address.

God, if he'd known she lived in such a dive, he would have been down here weeks ago. It wasn't safe for a woman to walk alone in this part of town. He'd passed a pile of syringes on the footpath as he'd looked for her apartment building, and he'd been offered two drug deals between parking his ute and reaching the main street.

The noise of the weekend traffic was so loud he could barely think, and it had been a pleasure to step into the building where the noise lowered to a muted roar. God, if Lucy preferred living down here in what she had called a civilised environment maybe there wasn't a chance for them. Maybe they were two different people who were just sexually compatible?

No. If he believed that, he wouldn't be here. He pushed open the glass door at the bottom of the steps, walked up to the third floor, and stood outside the door marked Apartment Nine. Garth took a deep breath and raised his hand to knock.

CHAPTER 25

Lucy stood with the freezer door open, debating whether to take out the frozen packet of Satay Chicken or Spaghetti Bolognese. The spaghetti won.

Once she'd admitted to herself that she really didn't want to be in the city, she had some big decisions to make. Her initial reaction had been to flee straight home—because she admitted now, the Pilliga Scrub was home, no matter how the city had sucked her in over the past few years. It had been a way of coping with Mum and Dad's deaths, and the six weeks at Prickle Creek Farm had woken her up to that fact. She'd been totally miserable since she'd come back to Sydney, but even though she'd admitted that to herself. She couldn't go running back to Garth. He didn't want her.

She opened the door of the microwave and shoved the frozen dinner on the glass plate just as someone knocked at the door. She frowned and wondered who it was. Seb had gone back to the farm, and Jemima was in Melbourne at the Myers fashion show. She was going from Melbourne to the farm for her three-month stay.

Company was the last thing she wanted tonight. She'd lost touch with her girlfriends while she'd been away, but tonight Jenny, her closest friend in Sydney, had called to see if Lucy wanted to go to the movies. She had declined—too much thinking to do. She ignored the loneliness. She'd gotten used to that.

Lucy crossed cautiously to the door and listened, jumping back as the door rattled when someone knocked again.

'Who is it?' she called.

'It's me. Garth. Open the door, Luce; it stinks out here.'

What?

'Garth?'

Lucy put her hand to her mouth as a maelstrom of emotions surged through her.

Joy. Confusion. Panic. Happiness and dread fought for precedence as she flicked the lock over.

Garth?

She was thinking about him, and he'd come knocking at her damn door?

The door opened, and she peered around it. The joy surging through her pushed away every other feeling clamouring inside her. She stepped back, and Garth stepped into her apartment. She drank in the sight of him as her heart almost pounded out of her chest.

Garth stared at her, his beautiful lips breaking into a broad smile. 'Hello, Lucy-Lou,' he said softly. 'I came to say sorry.'

Lucy shook her head, unable to believe that Garth was in her flat.

'You took your time,' she said dryly.

'I didn't think you wanted me anymore. I was leaving you in peace.'

'What made you change your mind?' She pointed to the couch and waited till he sat, pushing down the emotion. All she wanted to do was jump into his arms, but she had to be sure.

Lucy sat down beside him, her hands folded in her lap. Disbelief filled her, and she unclenched her hands as Garth held out his hand to her. She watched as he took her hand in his and lifted it to his lips. Joy shot through her and settled in her chest.

'What made me change my mind?' His voice was quiet, and he didn't take his eyes off her.' How long have I got?'

'As long as it takes.' She kept the smile from her voice, but it was hard to stay calm.

'First off, the brightness has gone out of my days—and nights. The farm work is just a chore without you there, there's no reason to go out and work. There's no one to look forward to seeing. The bottom line is, Lucy, I can't go on like that.' His eyes were intent as he looked around the room. 'When I move to Sydney, we're going to have to find a better place to live.'

'When you move to Sydney?' she repeated, but her voice was shaking as much as the rest of her.

Garth raised his other hand and cupped her cheeks in his palms. The rough pad of one thumb rubbed gently over her lips. 'If that's what it takes to be with you, that's what I'll do.'

Lucy closed her eyes as his words washed over her.

'I love you, Lucy. I'm not letting you go. No matter what it takes, I'll follow you wherever you want to be.'

She opened her eyes and met Garth's loving gaze.

'No matter what it takes,' he repeated. 'I can get work down here.'

'You mean you would move to the city for me?' Joy pulsed through her body in time with her fast-beating heart.

'I'll do anything to make you happy. Anything to be where you are.'

'You don't have to do that.' Finally, she let the smile cross her face. 'I was going to come home, anyway.'

'Home?' His voice held a smidgeon of hope. 'Home to where?'

'Home to Prickle Creek Farm.' She shook her head. 'No, not Prickle Creek Farm. Home to the Mackenzie Farm. If the farmer will have me?'

'If I'll have you?' Garth clutched both her hands in his and stared at her. She'd forgotten how beautiful his eyes were. And they were even more beautiful as his eyes held hers, full of love. Are you sure, Lucy?'

'I've never been so sure of anything in my life. I love you, Garth.' Lucy lifted her hand from his and placed it on his cheek.

Garth's arms went around her as she hugged him, and they fell back onto the sofa together. 'I can't believe it. Are you really, really sure?'

'I think I hate the city,' she said with a smile.

'I thought you loved your Thai restaurant?' His grin was huge. 'Not that I mind one bit. I've been teaching myself to cook Thai . . . and Japanese.'

Lucy caught the look of love on Garth's face just before his lips took hers in a kiss that sealed her future.

Their future.

EPILOGUE

Jemmy made Lucy sit at the table to shell the peas from Gran's veggie patch for the minted green pea salad.

'Liam, will you go and pick me a lemon?' she called out to the verandah where the men were making a racket.

'No, I'm busy.'

Jemmy rolled her eyes and headed outside to the veggie patch where the lemon tree shaded Gran's tomatoes from the last of the summer heat.

Gran watched her as she ran across the yard and turned to Lucy with a smile. 'Where did the fashion model go?'

Lucy grinned. 'I can't believe she's taken up her teaching course again. She's only got one subject to go, and she'll graduate. She didn't need to, you know. She's selling her unit on the harbour.'

'I couldn't believe she'd dropped that course when she was so close to finishing it,' Gran said. 'She could have been out here in the local school all this time instead of swanning around the world modelling clothes.'

'Oh, come on, Gran, don't be an old prickle.' Lucy's lips twitched as she waited for Gran's response.

'Well, I've been called lots of cranky names, but that's a first.' Her grandmother's mouth dropped open, and she burst out laughing. 'And you're right, Jemima will be a wonderful bridesmaid tomorrow.'

Lucy couldn't believe that tomorrow was going to be her wedding day. The day that she and Garth would start their lives together. 'I'm going to be a bride, Gran.'

'A beautiful bride,' Gran said. 'I'm so pleased you decided to have the wedding out here at Prickle Creek Farm.'

'And I'm so pleased I've got the best caterer in the west doing the catering.'

'Even with your grandfather wanting Lattice Slice for the dessert?' Gran laughed as she placed a plastic bride and groom in the middle of a huge tray of the creamy slice.

Lucy pushed herself to her feet and walked to the window. Pop was on the verandah issuing directions to Seb, Liam, and Garth, who were up three ladders pinning fairy lights along the edge of the verandah roof. She walked across to Gran as Jemmy walked in with an armful of lemons.

LUCY

Lucy pulled her grandmother in for a hug and held Jemmy's gaze as she spoke softly.

'Listen, Gran. Close your eyes and listen. Can you hear it?'

'Hear what, love?' Gran tipped her head to the side.

'I can hear Mum, and Aunty Jean, and Aunty Carol laughing. They're here with us in spirit.' Lucy smiled as a feeling of peace settled on her, and Jemmy's eyes filled with tears as she smiled across the room at her. She dropped the lemons into the sink and walked over to join the group hug.

'You're right, love. So can I,' said Gran. Her voice softened, and her faded eyes glowed with a happy smile. 'So can I.'

Garth was watching them through the large sliding glass door, and his teeth flashed as he smiled at her. A warm feeling curled in Lucy's stomach, and she smiled as Garth blew her a kiss.

Lucy had come home to Prickle Creek, and tomorrow she would be Garth's wife, and finally, she acknowledged to herself what coming home meant.

It didn't matter if there was red dust or prickles.

Or smelly cattle and hot winds.

Home was where your heart was, and Lucy's was very firmly entrenched at Prickle Creek Farm.

With Garth Mackenzie...and the rest of her beautiful family.

Love you, she mouthed to him over the top of Gran's head.

'Love you back,' Garth called.

THE END

LUCY

Liam's story is next. Come and meet Angie:

Angie Edmonds is content with life in the small town of Prickle Creek. Being alone doesn't bother her until Liam Smythe, the man who broke her heart, shows up at her vet clinic with an injured puppy. Unfortunately, he's just as irresistible as she remembers. In an attempt to prove to him that she's moved on, somehow a little white lie begins . . .

When Liam returns to help run the family farm, his enjoyment of the slow life in Prickle Creek surprises him. After all, he's used to the thrill of chasing the next big story. Running into the girl he's never been able to forget is unexpected, and he's shocked to learn she's getting married—to someone who's not him. She's off-limits, but Liam can't stop thinking about the gorgeous vet and what could have been. But convincing her he's changed will be harder than finding a needle in a haystack.

ANNIE SEATON

ANGIE:

eBook:
https://books2read.com/u/38qjlV

Print:
https://annieseatonstore.ecwid.com/Angie-A-Prickle-Creek-Romance-PRE-ORDER-February-p712102286

NOTE:
Previously published in the US as *Her Outback Surprise.*

LUCY

GRAN'S PRICKLE FARM

RECIPES

ANNIE SEATON

A CHOCOLATE CAKE JUST LIKE GRAN USED TO MAKE . . .

From the CWA Cakes Cookbook.

Ingredients
2 cups self-raising flour
3 tablespoons cocoa
1 1/2 cups sugar
1 1/2 cups milk
2 eggs
2 tablespoons butter, melted

Method
Sift flour and cocoa into a bowl
Add the sugar, milk and eggs and beat well
Add the melted butter and beat for another two minutes
Pour into a tin (the recipe does not specify; use your common sense!) and bake in an oven at 180 degrees Celsius for 1 hour

Icing
Chocolate Cream Cheese Frosting
from *Donna Hay* Magazine

Ingredients
100g butter

LUCY

500g cream cheese
2 cups (320g icing sugar)
1/2 cup (50g) cocoa

Method

Beat butter and cream cheese until pale and creamy

Add the icing sugar and cocoa and beat for 6-8 minutes until light and fluffy

Ice your damn cake!

ANNIE SEATON

POP'S FAVOURITE LATTICE SLICE

3 teaspoons gelatine
1/3 cup water
1 cup caster sugar
400g cream cheese at room temperature
100g butter at room temperature
3 tablespoons lemon juice
2 lemons, zested
1 teaspoon vanilla essence
2 packets Arnott's Lattice biscuits

Method

Dissolve gelatine in lukewarm water. Allow to stand.

Beat together sugar and cream cheese. Add softened butter until combined. Mix through lemon juice, rind and vanilla essence. Once combined, add the gelatine mixture and beat well.

In a baking dish or cake tin, place one packet of biscuits to cover the bottom layer completely. Use only whole biscuits. Pour the filling over the biscuit layer. Then, using the other packet of biscuits, place them directly over the top of the biscuits from the bottom layer (this will enable easy cutting). Cover and refrigerate until set.

Cut into squares, as per the biscuit layout.

GRAN'S MINTED PEA SALAD

200g shelled fresh peas
200g sugar snap peas, topped
200g small snow peas, topped
100g pea shoots (see note)
2 cups mint leaves
200g low-fat feta cheese
1 garlic clove, crushed with salt
2 tablespoons lemon juice
1 teaspoon honey
100ml extra virgin olive oil
1 tablespoon dried mint

Method

For the dressing, combine the crushed garlic, lemon juice and honey. Slowly whisk in the extra virgin olive oil. Stir in the mint and season with black pepper.

In a large pan of boiling salted water, cook fresh peas for 5-6 minutes (3 minutes if frozen), adding the sugar snap and snow peas for the final 2 minutes. Drain and refresh under cold water. Cool completely.

Place the vegetables in a large bowl with the pea shoots, feta, mint and dressing and toss gently to combine.

ALSO BY ANNIE SEATON

Daughters of the Darling
From Across the Sea
Over the River
By the Billabong (2025)
A Bec Whitfield Mystery
Bowen River
Shadows on the Shore (June 2025)
Duckinwilla Days
Coming Home
Secrets and Surprises
Books 3-7 to follow in 2025
Home to the Outback (2025)
Lucy
Angie
Jemima
Isabella
Porter Sisters Series
Kakadu Sunset
Daintree
Diamond Sky
Hidden Valley
Larapinta
Kakadu Dawn
Others
Whitsunday Dawn

ANNIE SEATON

Undara
Osprey Reef
East of Alice
One Summer in Tuscany
Four Seasons Short and Sweet
Follow the Sun
Ten Days in Paradise
Deadly Secrets
Adventures in Time
Silver Valley Witch
The Emerald Necklace
A Clever Christmas
Christmas with the Boss
Her Christmas Star
The Emerald Necklace

The Augathella Girls Series

Outback Roads
Outback Sky
Outback Escape
Outback Wind
Outback Dawn
Outback Moonlight
Outback Dust
Outback Hope

Boxed Sets

Augathella Girls 1-4
Augathella Girls 5-8

Augathella Short and Sweet Series
An Augathella Surprise
An Augathella Baby
An Augathella Spring
An Augathella Christmas
An Augathella Wedding
An Augathella Easter
An Augathella Masquerade Ball
<u>Boxed Set</u>
Augathella Short and Sweet 1-3
Sunshine Coast Series
Waiting for Ana
The Trouble with Jack
Healing His Heart
Sunshine Coast Books 1-3
The Richards Brothers Series
The Trouble with Paradise
Marry in Haste
Outback Sunrise
Richards Brothers Books 1-3
Bondi Beach Love Series
Beach House
Beach Music
Beach Walk
Beach Dreams
The House on the Hill <u>*Books 1-4*</u>
Second Chance Bay Series

ANNIE SEATON

Her Outback Playboy
Her Outback Protector
Her Outback Haven
Her Outback Paradise
<u>Boxed Set</u>
The McDougalls of Second Chance Bay <u>**Books 1-4**</u>
Love Across Time Series
Come Back to Me
Follow Me
Finding Home
The Threads that Bind
<u>Boxed Set</u>
Love Across Time 1-4
Bindarra Creek
Worth the Wait
Full Circle
Secrets of River Cottage
A Clever Christmas
A Place to Belong

Annie lives in Australia, on the beautiful north coast of New South Wales. She sits in her writing chair and looks out over the tranquil Pacific Ocean.

She writes contemporary romance and loves telling stories that always have a happily ever after. She lives with her very own hero of many years and they share their home with Barney, the rag doll puss, who hides when the four grandchildren come to visit.

Stay up to date with her latest releases at her website: **http://www.annieseaton.net**

If you would like to stay up to date with Annie's releases, subscribe to her newsletter here: **http://www.annieseaton.net**

www.ingramcontent.com/pod-product-compliance
Ingram Content Group UK Ltd.
Pitfield, Milton Keynes, MK11 3LW, UK
UKHW040738270125
454275UK00001B/112